VOLUME ONE:
THE JUNIOR NOVELIZATION

Adapted by Steve Behling
Cover illustrated by Patrick Spaziante

Random House 🏠 New York

CHAPTER ONE

"**A**w, crud!"

Darius Bowman had been playing the new Jurassic World video game for days now, trying to reach the end. And just when he thought he was going to beat the thing once and for all, he was eaten by Velociraptors.

The twelve-year-old sat in his bedroom, slumped in the seat by his video game, defeated.

Suddenly: "RAAAAAAAAARRRRRR!"

"Gah!!!!" Darius shouted, startled by the roar. He whirled around in his seat, only to find his older brother, Brandon, smiling at him.

"Not cool, Brand," Darius said grumpily.

"Aw, c'mon, man," Brand said, looking at the video game screen. "The dinos get you every time."

Darius rolled his eyes, reached over, and picked up the game's user guide. Brand smiled and threw himself down onto Darius's bed.

"Brand, I'm so close! If I can just get around the T. rex, I beat the game and win the—"

"Trip to Jurassic World. I know. You've said it, like, a thousand times," Brand sighed. "But if straight-up gamers say this thing's unwinnable, how's some dino-nerd kid gonna beat it?"

Darius looked at the manual for a second and shrugged his shoulders. "Great pep talk, bro."

"Look, Darius," Brand began. "I know getting to Jurassic World was your and Dad's dream. But there's more to life than just dinosaurs. You never leave your room anymore, bruh. Dad wouldn't want this."

"I hear you," Darius said quietly. "But . . . even if winning is dumb and hopeless, I still gotta try."

Brand looked at his brother, and his expression softened. "Can ya at least take a break? Maybe work in a shower? You're smelling pretty funky, man."

Darius laughed. He couldn't stay mad at his brother for long.

As Brand left the room, Darius turned toward a photo of himself with his dad. He missed him.

They all did.

"That's it!" Darius shouted, waking up from a dead sleep. He rummaged through his dinosaur reference books. He had all the important ones, like Dr. Ellie

Sattler's *Botany of the Late Cretaceous* and Dr. Ian Malcolm's *God Creates Dinosaurs.*

"Attack patterns," Darius mumbled to himself, searching through the books. "No . . . vocalizations . . . pack behavior . . . no . . . got it!"

He was holding Dr. Alan Grant's book *The Lost World of the Dinosaurs* in his hands and flipped through it feverishly.

YES! he thought. *This might be it!*

He carried the book over to his computer and put on the VR headset. Then he booted up the game. The screen read RESTART FROM WAYPOINT.

A T. rex with enormous, menacing jaws was coming right for him. Darius's game avatar rolled out of the way, narrowly avoiding the hungry beast.

"Whereareyouwhereareyou?" Darius mumbled, frantically searching the ground for something he remembered having seen before. "Where are you?"

And then he saw it—a Raptor skull.

Darius pressed ACTIVATE RAPTOR SKULL.

"Please whistle," Darius whispered.

Or I'm gonna be dead. For, like, the millionth time.

At last, a sound came out of the Raptor skull. Not just a sound. A whistle. Some kind of call.

Two Raptors came running, attracted by the

sound. Hissing, they leaped onto the bigger dinosaur, the dangerous sickle-shaped claws on each of their hind feet slashing. The T. rex roared, trying to shake them off.

It was the break Darius needed! His avatar jumped into a helicopter, and Darius watched as the scene dissolved before his eyes—only to be replaced by the ginormous, imposing gates of Jurassic World itself.

"Congratulations, player!"

The voice belonged to Mr. DNA, a cartoon character who acted as a guide in the video game. "I'm Mr. DNA! You're the first person to *ever* beat our game. So we wanna reward you—with a trip to Jurassic World's brand-new, state-of-the-art adventure camp! That's right! Get ready to join us—at Camp Cretaceous!"

Darius sat in stunned silence, staring at the screen as the Camp Cretaceous logo flashed. It took a few seconds for his brain to catch up.

"BRAND- . . . MOM!!!!!" Darius hollered with uncontrollable excitement.

"Welcome to Isla Nublar, campers!"

Darius had just stepped off the ferry, his legs only a little rubbery from the wave-tossed ride from the mainland to Isla Nublar. He stood on the dock, hardly hearing the person speaking to the group. He couldn't believe he was really here! Jurassic World! Dinosaurs! His dad's dream. *His* dream! He quickly reached up to rub the Velociraptor tooth necklace his father had given him. Immediately, he felt his dad's presence when he touched the fossil. He smiled.

"You are the chosen few, the first kids in the *entire world* to ever experience the awesomeness that is Camp Cretaceous!" said the man standing in front of him.

Darius had been so excited that he hadn't even introduced himself to the four other kids who were standing on the dock with him.

"I know the trip from the mainland was rough on some," the man said. "Hello, Ben . . ."

Darius looked over at the kid standing next to him who gave a nervous thumbs-up to the man before bending over, obviously about to lose his lunch.

Guess that's Ben, Darius thought.

"But ya made it! I'm Dave, head counselor," the man said.

Before Dave could say another word, a large vehicle broke through the brush in the distance, its horn honking wildly. The 6x4 skidded to a stop right in front of Darius and the other kids.

"Ahh!" said a woman leaping out of the vehicle. "So sorry I'm late! Welcome, campers! I'm Roxie, head counselor of Camp Cretaceous!"

Darius swiveled to look at "Head Counselor"

Dave. The other kids did the same.

"Well," Dave laughed, "it's sort of a 'co-head counselor' sorta situation."

"Is it?" Roxie asked cheerfully.

Darius noticed that one of the kids was recording the moment with her phone.

Dave cleared his throat loudly, then said, "Anyway! Some of you won contests to be here, some of you had VIP invites, but for the next two weeks, *all* of you will be getting the five-star treatment."

"As our first campers, we've lined up exclusive behind-the-scenes tours of Jurassic World," Roxie said. "There's also kayaking, rock climbing, obstacle courses, and . . . of course . . ."

"DINOSAURS!?" Darius said, his mouth apparently operating independently of his brain. His cheeks felt hot as Roxie looked at him over her clipboard, smiling.

"Yes, Darius, plenty of dinosaurs," she said. "So, ready for an adventure?"

Before Darius could respond, another kid—the one who had been filming—said, "Absolutely! But I'm gonna need that speech a little shorter, and really try to lean into the *majesty* of this place."

Dave just ignored her. "Okay, we're going now!" he said brightly. "Let's get the six of you to camp!"

Ben, free from his nausea for a moment, raised his hand and said, "Uh, there are five of us?"

"Where *is* six?" Dave asked.

Just then came the sound of a helicopter landing nearby, kicking up dirt and dust.

"Greetings, my dudes!" said a tall guy stepping out of the helicopter. He was carrying a duffel bag as he walked toward the group. "Kenji is here, so let the party commence!"

Kenji shoved his bag into Roxie's arms. "Put this in my room," Kenji said. Clearly irritated, Roxie blew a stray strand of hair out of her face.

As the new boy strutted by, Darius wondered, *What's his deal?*

Then Roxie tossed the bag right back at Kenji, catching him in the stomach.

"Okay!" she announced cheerfully. "Let's go!"

CHAPTER TWO

The 6x4 headed down a hill with Roxie at the steering wheel, making some hairpin turns. The kids were thrown left and right. Darius could have sworn that Ben was literally turning green.

"What's good, Brooklanders?" said the girl with the phone. She filmed herself constantly. "It's your girl, Brooklynn, coming at you from the best place ever—Camp Cretaceous! Like and subscribe to join me, as I . . . *unbox Jurassic World.*"

Brooklynn turned to face the other kids in the vehicle. "Okay, I need you all to say who you are and a little about yourself. *Aaaaaaand* . . . ACTION!"

Before Darius even had a chance to object, Brooklynn's phone was in his face. "Oh! Um . . . I beat this awesome VR dinosaur game. I'm Darius, by the—"

"I'm sorry," said another girl, abruptly cutting off

Darius. "I just can't believe—you're Brooklynn! I'm Sammy Gutierrez, *total* Brooklander! Oh, also, my family supplies all the beef for the Park and that's how I got here!"

Brooklynn smiled at the girl and said, "Great to meet you, Sammy!"

"Uh . . . what's a 'Brooklander'?" Darius asked.

"Oh, that's just what my online followers call themselves," Brooklynn replied.

"Uh, all twenty-seven million of us!" Sammy added excitedly.

"Yep!" said another girl. "That's why she's the only one who gets to keep her cell phone. She's 'famous.' "

And at just that moment, Ben finally threw up.

Darius thought the jungle on Isla Nublar was simply incredible. All the books he'd read, all the documentaries he'd seen—none of them had done it justice. He scanned the bushes as they drove through the jungle, hoping to see signs of dinosaurs.

"Hold on!" Roxie shouted, hitting the brakes. The kids were flung forward against their seat belts.

The counselors jumped out of the vehicle.

"Um, Dave?" Ben asked meekly after being jostled by the sudden stop. "What's going on?"

"Nothing you need to worry about!" Dave said, sounding super upbeat.

This made Ben worry even more than he already had been worrying.

"But you should all definitely stay in your seats."

That made everyone unbuckle their seat belts and leap to the side of the vehicle to see what was going on.

Darius noticed that both Dave and Roxie were holding long pole-like objects in their hands. He recognized them as stun spears, which were almost standard issue among the people who worked at Jurassic World. The stun spears could momentarily stop a dinosaur without hurting them.

Dave, Roxie, and the kids were all on edge, waiting for something to happen. Darius turned his head a little, then noticed some plants moving slightly.

"Guys?" he said, trying to get everyone's attention. "Guys?"

No one had so much as looked at Darius, when a Compsognathus leaped from the brush and into the 6x4!

The small, turkey-sized dinosaur skittered around the back of the vehicle, and the kids screamed. Darius fell over onto his back and noticed Kenji hiding behind Brooklynn.

Darius felt something land on his stomach, and

he looked up to see the Compy staring right at him.

My first real dinosaur! Darius thought. *Up close and in person! This is unbelievable!*

But before he could get a good look, Roxie threw a blanket over the Compy. Immediately, the small dinosaur seemed to calm down. Roxie placed the dinosaur in a what looked like a pet carrier.

"Crisis averted," Roxie said with a grin. "These things are ALWAYS getting out of their enclosure."

"A real live Compsognathus!" Darius said, still not quite believing it.

Kenji rolled his eyes. "Oh, please. Took a blanket AND a cat carrier to catch it. BOR-ing."

"Scared *you* pretty good," Darius said.

Kenji scowled as the other kids tried really hard not to smile. Brooklynn took a pic, capturing the moment.

"Welcome to Camp Cretaceous!" Dave said grandly as the kids looked up at the massive gates.

Camp Cretaceous was amazing!

The camp seemed to be a part of the jungle itself. It looked kind of like Jurassic World—the buildings reminded Darius of all the photos he'd seen, and especially the VR game.

One of the girls, an athletic-looking kid named

Yasmina, was looking around, too. *She seems nearly as impressed as me,* Darius thought.

Brooklynn, on the other hand, was documenting the moment on her phone. She slipped right in front of Yasmina, pointing the phone in her face. The girl's face fell, and she appeared uncomfortable.

"Yasmina!" Brooklynn shouted. "Hey, girl! So, as an elite athlete, how pumped are you for camp?"

"Elite athlete?" Darius thought. *Oh, right. Dave called her "Track Girl" before.*

"Not a huge fan of being on camera," Yasmina said, walking off.

"This place is almost as big as my family's ranch back home!" Sammy said.

"When we're up and running, the camp will house five hundred kids and a hundred and fifty staff," Roxie said.

Then Dave said, "Listen up! Announcement time!"

"Okay, everyone, there're some ground rules to cover," Roxie said. "Curfew is at eight p.m., and lights out is at nine p.m. sharp. This is for your safety. We are in a dinosaur-filled jungle! They're amazing, but they are *wild animals.* You must always keep your distance or you could be seriously hurt, if not worse."

"Define 'worse,' " Ben said.

"Cabins are up thataway," Dave said, and he pointed to what looked like the world's most advanced tree houses, nestled into trees. Suspension bridges connected one tree house to another. It was obvious that no expense had been spared to make this the coolest camp in history! It was all above ground—and all just for them!

"First one there gets top bunk!" Yasmina shouted, and "Track Girl" was off and running, pushing by Kenji.

It was now a free-for-all, no-holds-barred race for the elevator, with each of the kids vying for the best bunk.

Except Darius. He stayed behind, enthralled as he watched Roxie place the carrier containing the Compsognathus in a nearby truck.

"Get this lovely lady back to her pen," Roxie said to the driver. "Her family's probably worried sick."

The truck zoomed off as Darius hollered, "Wait! Aw, man, I *really* wanted to get a closer look."

"I like your enthusiasm, Darius," Dave said. "But right now it's 'claiming a bunk' time."

"But it's the first dinosaur I've ever seen in person and—"

A loud thumping echoed throughout the campground. Everything seemed to vibrate. Darius felt the thump in the pit of his stomach—it reminded him of that queasy feeling he would get on a roller coaster right as it dipped down a hill and came up another.

Then he looked at a puddle of water on the ground and saw it ripple.

Then came another THUMP.

"Oh, the day is not over, buddy," Dave said with a grin.

"There's a Brachiosaurus!" Darius practically screamed. "Parasaurolophus! Stegosaurus! Ankylosaurus!"

The group had traveled from camp to a huge observation tower overlooking the valley below. Atop the platform, Darius saw an amazing panorama of Isla Nublar, the sun setting in the distance.

The dinosaurs in the valley were the source of all the thumping Darius had experienced back at camp.

Then Darius saw something that made his eyes pop out of his skull. "Are those Sinoceratops?" he said, pointing. "When did you get those?"

Dave chuckled. "They're cooking up all kinds of new dinos in the lab."

Darius watched as a herd of dinosaurs was being led by Camp Cretaceous workers riding all-terrain vehicles.

"Whoa!" Sammy said. "Where are they herding them to?"

"They're herding them back to their nighttime enclosures," Roxie explained.

"Enough banter!" Dave said. "It's zip-line party time!"

"Maybe Yasmina should go first," Ben said as he was strapped into the zip-line harness. He teetered atop the edge of the zip-line tower, doing his best to defy gravity and physics and remain on the tower. "Or anyone? I really don't—"

Before Ben could protest any further, Dave clapped the kid on his back, sending him down the zip line.

Ben screamed the whole way down, and so did the other kids. Except the other kids screamed the "Woo-hoo! This is so cool!!!" kind of screams, while Ben's scream was more like "This is all a colossal mistake, and I am going to die!"

Darius couldn't wait for his turn on the zip line. From the moment he went over the edge and zoomed above the forest below, he was awestruck. Below him, birds were flying. As Darius got closer to the ground, he felt like he was one of the dinosaurs! He even made eye contact with a Brachiosaurus on the way down. Darius wondered, *Can anything top this experience?*

CHAPTER THREE

When the kids got back to camp, they were exhausted. They all wanted to go to sleep so they could see what surprises tomorrow would bring.

Everyone, that was, except Darius. He was awake, looking out the window at a dinosaur enclosure. He snuck out of his bunk and into the common room on his way out of the tree house.

Until his father had passed away, it had been their dream to come to Jurassic World—not just to see the dinosaurs, but to *be* with the dinosaurs. And now those prehistoric creatures they had obsessed over were *so* close. Leaving the camp would be crazy, but—

"Hey there, Dino Nerd," Kenji said, yawning. "Whatcha doin'?"

"Huh?" Darius said, trying to think fast. "Nothing. I was just . . . uh . . . heading out . . . 'cause . . . thirsty."

Kenji's eyes didn't leave Darius, and he pointed at a nearby watercooler.

"Look, bro," Kenji said, putting his arm around Darius's shoulders. "I don't want you to be intimidated by me just because I'm rich, my father owns a few condos on the island, and I'm rich."

"I'm not intimidated by you," Darius replied sincerely.

"Oh, good!" Kenji said. "I want us to be friends. And friends tell each other stuff—for instance, what they're doing out of bed after curfew."

"I think you best get your arm off me, *friend*," Darius said, his anger rising.

"Oh. Why don't you make me, *friend*?"

"Huh," Brooklynn said from the doorway. "So this is what toxic masculinity looks like."

"Sorry we woke you," Darius said. "I—"

"He was sneaking out," Kenji said. "But I set him straight. I try to look out for younger kids."

"I've been waiting my whole life to get here," Darius said. "And I'm gonna make the most of it."

Then he pointed at the window, toward the dinosaur enclosure. "Those lights must be coming from the Compy enclosure. I just gotta check it out!"

Darius watched as Brooklynn raised an eyebrow and fiddled with her phone. "Sneaking out to see dinosaurs in the dead of night, mad danger of getting caught, great mood lighting . . . I guess that means . . . it's a late-night dino exclusive, Brooklanders! We're going rogue!"

"Shhhh!" Brooklynn said to her camp mates as a worker next to the enclosure turned his head. Not hearing anything, the worker kept on moving. Then a truck left the enclosure.

Soon, Darius, Kenji, and Brooklynn were walking along a gangplank above the dinosaur enclosure. If they had been just a little lower, they would have seen this sign below them: WARNING: EXTREME DANGER.

"Hey, Brooklynn!" Kenji said in a loud whisper. "You can get a good shot from over here. Allow me!"

"No thanks," Brooklynn replied. "I can—"

Kenji reached for the phone. Brooklynn tried to keep her grip on it, but the phone fell onto the walkway below with a metallic clang.

"Thanks, Kenji," Brooklynn said. "Real smooth."

"Relax. I'll get it," Kenji said.

Darius protested, but Kenji swung over the railing and climbed down the bars to the walkway below. Then he picked up the phone.

"See?" Kenji said. "Good as new."

Brooklynn looked furious. "Great. Now just climb back up and *gently* hand it to me."

"Sure, sure," Kenji said. "Right after I get a sweet dino pic for your followers."

Darius looked at the Compsognathus pen. Something was wrong. For one thing, there were a lot of footprints on the ground that looked bigger than a Compy's. For another, there were claw marks on the trees and a big pile of bones on the ground.

"Guys, this isn't the Compy pen!" Darius whispered urgently.

"Quiet, junior!" Kenji said loudly. "The grown-ups are talking."

Then Kenji stuck his arm through the bars of the enclosure with the phone, taking pictures.

"Ah, your followers are gonna love this! Here, Compy Compy Compy!" Kenji said.

"THIS ISN'T THE COMPY PEN!" Darius hissed as loudly as he dared.

Kenji's arm was still inside the enclosure when the first Velociraptor appeared.

Stunned, Kenji still managed to take a picture with Brooklynn's phone. The flash angered the Raptor, who charged. Falling back, Kenji yanked his arm away from the bars as the Raptor slammed into them.

"Open the gate!" Kenji shouted. He yanked hard on the doors that led out of the enclosure, but they wouldn't budge.

Darius looked down and saw a control panel. But he had no idea which button would open the doors to free Kenji!

Brooklynn didn't, either. But that didn't stop her from slamming one of the buttons with her hand. Suddenly, lights flashed, sirens blared, and doors started to open.

Except they weren't the doors that led out of the enclosure. They were the doors separating Kenji from the Raptor. Now there was nothing between Kenji and his would-be attacker.

Looking down, Darius saw an exhaust pipe right by the Raptor. Kicking down hard, he managed to dislodge the pipe, releasing a blast of white-hot steam on the Raptor!

Leaping down, Darius hit the ground, landing near Kenji.

The steam drifted off, revealing the Raptor was still there. Except she was joined by three more Raptors. And they all looked hungry.

"It's okay, it's okay . . . ," Darius repeated. "We're all okay. . . ."

Behind him, Kenji cowered, as Darius stood between him and the ferocious Raptors. Darius's palms were up, like he was trying to say to the dinosaurs, "Hey, easy, guys."

"Kenji," Darius said, not taking his eyes off the Raptors, "those bones . . . check for a Raptor skull."

He nodded toward a nearby pile of dinosaur bones.

"What?" Kenji said, as if Darius had just asked him to stick his hand in an unflushed toilet.

"In the video game, I—"

One of the Raptors, the one who seemed to be their leader, got closer, snapping and hissing. Blue and silver marking started at its yellow eyes and went down each side of its body. Alarmed, Darius flinched, tripping and falling over a branch.

The Raptors were drawing closer and were practically on top of Darius. He still held his hands up, but they were shaking.

Suddenly, there was a brilliant flash. All around the enclosure, floodlights turned on!

Now it was the Raptors' turn to flinch. They hissed and closed their eyes to the bright lights.

"Hey! Come and get it!"

It was Roxie! Darius looked up and saw her standing next to Brooklynn. She had something in her hands and tossed it into the enclosure toward the Raptors. The dinosaurs scrambled for the thick slab of meat she had thrown in.

"Get outta there!" Roxie ordered, as Dave burst into the enclosure. He grabbed both kids and dashed out before the Raptors could lose interest in the cold meat.

The door to the enclosure slammed shut.

"Dave, that was . . . ," Darius started. He wasn't sure what he should say. "You were amazing. Thank you so much."

"Standard procedure, Darius," Dave said, smiling as if it was an everyday occurrence. He continued to grin for another moment before turning around and throwing up in the bushes.

"Are you hurt?" Roxie asked, ignoring Dave and rushing over to Darius and Kenji. "Is everyone all right?"

Dave held up a hand to indicate that he was fine, but Roxie was only focused on the kids.

Darius was about to say something when he noticed Kenji trying to sneak away. Roxie grabbed him by the shoulder. "Whoa, whoa, whoa, whoa! Where do you think you're going?"

Then she spun Kenji around, and she stared him in the face. "You and Darius are in *big* trouble."

"I . . . I . . . But he was—" Darius stuttered.

"Save it," Roxie said, cutting him off. "We'll decide what to do with you later. If you even *get* to remain here after a stunt like this."

Darius couldn't believe it. After all the years of wanting to come to Jurassic World, to see dinosaurs, after playing that game for hours and hours, suddenly, it might all come to an end.

And it was all his fault.

Kenji sat on the couch in the common room, making annoying popping sounds with his mouth.

It was driving Darius nuts.

"How could you do something so stupid?" Darius said, losing it.

Kenji made the mouth-popping noise again. "Maybe it wasn't my best idea," he admitted. "Look, I don't want to get kicked out, either. When my dad . . ."

The mention of Kenji's father got Darius's attention, and he looked at the other kid.

"My whole life, I've been trying to make him proud," Kenji said. "If he finds out that I messed up again, he might . . . finally give up on me for good."

Darius didn't quite know what to say, when Roxie and Dave walked into the common room.

"We gave Brooklynn a warning for sneaking out," Dave began, "but what you two chuckleheads did—"

"Especially you, Kenji!" Roxie interjected. "Your recklessness put your, Darius's, *and* Dave's lives in danger! We should call your parents and tell them!"

"It was my fault!" Darius said, interrupting Roxie. "I jumped into the pit. Kenji was . . . trying to save me."

Kenji shot Darius a surprised look, then nodded, going along with it.

"I'm sorry," she said, not believing a word of it. "So *Darius,* the dino genius . . . was saved by Kenji, the kid who thinks dinosaurs went extinct because, and I quote, 'Their farts turned the air trashy.'"

"Prove me wrong, yo," Kenji said, shrugging.

Darius looked at Roxie. He didn't want to lie to her. But under the circumstances, he didn't know what else to do.

Roxie looked into Darius's eyes. He couldn't meet her gaze.

"Look, no harm, no foul," Dave said. "Let's chalk the whole thing up to experience. Lessons, friendships . . . this is what camp's all about!"

"Fine," Roxie said, the tone of her voice suggesting that it was anything *but* fine. "But one more misstep . . ."

"I . . . *we* won't let you down," Darius said. "So . . . what are we doing tomorrow?"

"Enjoy cleaning this up, boys," Roxie said.

Darius and Kenji were standing just outside the campgrounds in an area where there was an enormous mound of Apatosaurus droppings.

Roxie handed shovels to the boys.

"We're going to the genetics lab," Roxie said, indicating the other kids who would be having more fun. As they headed for the 6x4, Brooklynn stopped for a second. She snapped a pic of Kenji and Darius standing in front of the dinosaur poop.

Then Dave tossed them a small bottle of something. Darius caught it. "Cologne," Dave said. "That'll help with the smell. The stench of dinosaur poo can really *linger.*"

Dejected, Darius could only watch as the others took off for the genetics lab.

"Gross," Kenji said, looking at the dinosaur poop on his shoe.

Welcome to Camp Cretaceous, Darius thought.

CHAPTER FOUR

While Darius and Kenji shoveled dinosaur dung, the other kids rumbled down the road in the 6x4. Ben sorted through his fanny pack as Brooklynn stared at her phone, thumbing through a series of videos she'd posted to Brooklynn Unboxes. Under each was a tally that represented the number of views.

Instead of going up, indicating more people were watching, the numbers were going down.

"I'm *still* dropping followers?" Brooklynn moaned.

"So what's your next video?" Sammy asked. "Oooh, maybe there're baby dino eggs in the lab. Everyone loves a baby video!"

"Whatever it is, it'll be *cool,*" Brooklynn said with confidence that she really wasn't feeling.

As Brooklynn fretted over her followers, Ben was getting ready for the big visit. He hummed as he squirted something on his hands, arms, and even the zipper of his fanny pack.

"Sanitizer," Ben said. "Who knows what kind of creepy dino goo is at that lab? You gotta be ready for anything."

The 6x4 arrived outside the genetics lab, and the kids got out, along with Roxie and Dave.

"What's good, Brooklanders?" Brooklynn said, filming. "Today, I'm coming to you from one of Jurassic World's *coolest* remote genetics labs, aka where the dinos are made!"

Brooklynn waved the phone around so her followers could see the large industrial building. The lab itself was hidden behind concrete pillars and metal grating.

"This is a rare window into the Park's inner workings," Roxie said to the kids. "Not just anyone can come h—"

"Doc Wu!" Dave shouted.

A neatly dressed dark-haired man in the lab—Dr. Wu—suddenly looked like he had eaten a lemon soaked in even more lemon. He pretended not to see Dave or the kids and just kept on walking.

Roxie shot Dave a look, then chased after the famed scientist. "We're here for the tour, Dr. Wu. Camp

Cretaceous? Ms. Dearing should've mentioned—"

"I'm sorry, but Mr. Masrani has accelerated the timetable for our newest exhibit yet again," Dr. Wu said, annoyed. "I simply don't have time to spend the afternoon babysitting *children*."

Sammy frowned, while Brooklynn filmed the doctor's outburst.

"Young lady, no recording in the lab!" Dr. Wu ordered.

"Sorry, Doctor. I just wanted my followers to meet the genius who brought dinosaurs back to life," Brooklynn said, making her eyes go wide with adoration.

Dr. Wu raised an eyebrow.

"I mean, without *you*, there is no Jurassic World. But hey, if you wanna toil in the shadows while Masrani and John Hammond get *all* the credit, I respect that. It's about the work."

Brooklynn could see that she had hit a nerve. Dr. Wu leaned in and asked, "How many people watch this web show of yours?"

"Thanks to you, I'm shoveling poop instead of watching a live dinosaur birth," Darius said. "That's only been my dream since, I don't know, *forever*!"

Darius dumped a shovelful of dung down a chute near a small containment tank. Instead of helping, Kenji was now squirting the cologne at insects like it was bug spray and swatting at big, fuzzy flies.

"It's cute you're excited about some dumb lab," Kenji said. "Newbs like you don't know the half of what's in this place."

"Like what?" Darius asked.

Kenji shrugged and smiled slyly. Like he was in on some big secret and Darius wasn't.

"I've been to this park, like, fifty kajillion times," Kenji said, swatting away a fly. "I'm in the know, junior. And since you helped me out earlier, I *might* be willing to show you the *good stuff.*"

Darius clasped the shovel handle tightly. "No," Darius said, shaking his head. "No way. I can't get into more trouble."

"Hey, suit yourself," Kenji said. "You've only been waiting a lifetime to see dinosaurs. I just thought you'd be interested in seeing one they stopped showing the public. It's only a once-in-a-lifetime opportunity."

Aw, crud, Darius thought.

"This tunnel is part of an underground network connecting the whole island," Kenji said. "*This* is how the big dogs get around."

Kenji held on to the sides of the ladder and slid down into the tunnel below.

"You're actually looking at a Jurassic World VIP, kid," Kenji said.

Unsure, but not wanting to miss an opportunity, Darius climbed down the ladder down carefully. He got the sense that this was a restricted area and definitely not part of any official activities that Roxie and Dave had planned for them—and that added to the excitement!

Behind him, the tunnel hatch closed with a loud CLANG. Darius hoped he wouldn't regret his decision.

While Brooklynn filmed Dr. Wu, Sammy pointed at a door in the distance.

"Dr. Wu?" Sammy asked. "What's *that*?"

Dr. Wu hissed. "It's *restricted*."

Meanwhile, Dave looked at an incubator filled with dinosaur eggs. "You guys, look!" he said. "I think one of the eggs is about to hatch!"

"That's not possible," Dr. Wu said, quite sure he was right. Except when he turned to look at the incubator, he realized that Dave was 100 percent right. An egg *was* hatching!

"That Ankylosaurus has only been incubating for ten weeks," Dr. Wu said, stunned.

As he looked at the egg, the shell cracked.

"Is that a foot?" Yasmina said, gasping.

It *was* a foot—coated in dinosaur goo. And when the leg kicked out of the shell, the goo splattered on Ben.

"Ew! Ew! Ew!" Ben said, freaking out. "Get it off me! Get it—"

Suddenly, the baby Ankylosaurus had broken free of its shell and tumbled out of the incubator. Instinctively, Ben reached out, catching the baby.

The Ankylosaurus tried to shake off a piece of shell that had stuck to her hide. But it wouldn't budge. To his surprise, and everyone else's, Ben removed the shell. The baby opened her eyes and cooed when she saw Ben.

Ben found himself relaxing at the sound.

"Sweet!" Brooklynn said, filming. "One of its head bumps is bigger than the other!"

"Asymmetry?" Dr. Wu said, horrified. "In *my* lab?"

However, nobody was listening to Dr. Wu. They were all too busy watching Ben make silly faces at the baby dinosaur.

In fact, everyone was so into it that they didn't even notice as Brooklynn stopped filming and slipped away from the group.

"Where are you taking me?" Darius asked.

As Darius looked around, he saw that the tunnel walls were lined with keypad controls. There were ladders on either side of the tunnel leading up to numbered paddocks.

"We're headed to where they quarantine the dinos that are too aggressive. The last one I saw here was some kind of carna . . . uh . . . Carna-something."

Darius clasped his hand over his mouth. "We're going to see a *Carnotaurus*?" he asked.

"Uh, obviously," Kenji said. "Like my boy Masrani always says, 'When Kenji promises, Kenji delivers!' "

Then he pressed a couple of buttons on a keypad and waited for the hatch above them to open.

It didn't.

Then Kenji pressed a few more buttons, and on the fourth or fifth try, the hatch opened. Darius couldn't help but smirk.

Brooklynn was sure no one had noticed that she had left the incubator room. She had walked down the hallway toward the door clearly marked RESTRICTED.

Looking around to make sure no one saw her, she was just about to open the door when she turned around and—BUMP—ran into Sammy!

"Oh, hey!" Sammy said brightly.

"Sammy, what are you doing out here?" Brooklynn asked.

"I was just . . . This place oughta come with a GPS," Sammy said. Then she leaned in close to Brooklynn and said, "I really gotta go."

"I think there's a bathroom on the other end of the hall, actually," Brooklynn said, trying to get rid of Sammy. "So . . ."

"Thanks," Sammy said. "See ya back there!"

Brooklynn watched as Sammy trotted off toward the bathroom, making sure that she was out of sight. Then Brooklynn tried to open the RESTRICTED door. But it was locked.

Out of the corner of her eye, Brooklynn saw Dr. Wu rounding the corner. She ducked behind a pillar and watched as he opened the door to his office.

Then a lab guy popped his head out. He looked excited and said, "Doctor! We have those results you were looking for, sir."

Wu turned around and walked back to the main lab with the other man.

Brooklynn watched the door slowly closing. Wu and the man disappeared, and just as the door was about to slam shut, Brooklynn caught it.

"Okay, Brooklanders," Brooklynn said. "Let's see if top-secret Jurassic World intel is *cool* enough for you."

Dr. Wu's lab was really dark, and she wondered how he could get any work done in a place like this. The only light seemed to come from a series of glowing test tubes. She could just make out a chalkboard across the room, filled with equations that Brooklynn couldn't make any sense of.

She walked over to a computer and jiggled the mouse. The home screen appeared, and she immediately noticed there were several folders on the desktop. Brooklynn clicked on the folders, reading the names out loud.

"E seven fifty. Clinical trial results," Brooklynn said. But her face brightened considerably when she read the name of the next folder. "Classified. *Jackpot!*"

She clicked on that folder, and that's when the screen flashed red, an ACCESS DENIED warning appeared, and a piercing alarm filled the room.

Then the computer screen went dark.

"Dang it," Brooklynn said. She knew she had to leave right away, but she saw something beneath a flash drive on the desk—an actual file folder that said INDOMINUS REX.

She was just about to open the folder when Dr. Wu slammed his hand down, keeping it closed.

Brooklynn managed a smile and said, "I thought the door said 'restroom.'"

"Where is that stupid fence?!?" Kenji complained. They had been wandering around in the dense jungle since exiting the tunnels.

"Kenji, maybe we should head back," Darius said. "We don't wanna get caught and cause you trouble with your dad."

"What does my dad have to do with anything? Dude's barely around. He's not worrying about me."

Darius stopped in his tracks and glared at Kenji. "What? Then what was all the 'My whole life, I've been trying to make my dad proud'?"

It took a second for it to click, and then Kenji said, "Oh, right. I was lying. 'Cause of the whole 'not wanting to get in trouble and sent home' thing."

Darius tried to think of something to say, but he was so angry, all he could do was stare at Kenji.

Shaking his head, Darius thought he was going to explode. "I can't believe this!" he shouted. "There *is* no Carnotaurus, is there?"

"Hey, I keep it honest!" Kenji said. "Except this morning. And, like, a bunch of other times today. But

I'm telling the truth about this!"

Darius was about to say something, but then came the roar.

THE ROAR.

Kenji pushed against a thick plant, revealing a huge metal fence that seemed to go on forever.

"Kenji delivers." The boy smiled and looked to see Darius's expression.

Darius didn't look excited.

He looked worried.

There was a loud THUMP of something coming closer.

"You know this park like the back of your hand, right?" Darius said.

"Uh, duh," Kenji replied.

"So you *definitely* know which side of the fence the Carnotaurus is on?"

That was actually something Kenji did *not* know. So it was something of a surprise when they turned around and saw the Carnotaurus right behind them!

CHAPTER FIVE

"Time for you all to leave," Dr. Wu said curtly.

Ben was trying to pry the baby dinosaur from him as he said, "But what about Bumpy?"

Dr. Wu grabbed hold of Bumpy and took him off Ben. "The *asset* will soon be released into a herd of Ankylosauruses. Then she'll be *their* problem, just like you all will cease to be *my* problem."

Roxie and Dave took the cue and hurried the kids out of the lab without saying a word.

On his way out, Ben turned to look at Bumpy. The little dinosaur pawed toward his new friend.

Then Dr. Wu slammed the door.

The Carnotaurus was right on their heels. It was similar to a T. rex, though not nearly as large—but totally capable of eating any campers that came its way. The dinosaur also had two distinct horns on its head that gave it a bullish look.

"Dude! It's gaining!" Kenji shouted.

Darius stared ahead, focused on one tree. "It's fast," he said, "but not on turns! Zigzag! On my count! One . . . two . . ."

Darius sprinted for the tree in the distance as the Carnotaurus followed. Just as he and Kenji were about to reach the tree—

"THREE!"

The boys went hard to the left. Unable to slow down in time, the Carnotaurus crashed right into the tree.

The boys ran, zigzagging all the way. The now dizzy Carnotaurus resumed the chase but was unsteady on its feet as it tried to keep up with all the sharp, sudden turns.

"Up ahead!" Darius called out, pointing to a metal gate. Kenji saw it and was the first one there. He jumped into the half-open gate, which was only about the size of a dog door. Somehow, he managed to wriggle and squirm his way through it, and Kenji emerged on the other side.

Behind him, Darius saw the Carnotaurus running for him.

Just as Darius squirmed into the gate, he bumped the side of the crawl space, causing the half-open gate to slam down on his back.

He was stuck, half in the crawl space, half out!

Darius tried to push the gate off of him, but it was just too heavy.

He was a sitting duck.

"Kenji!" Darius shouted.

But there was no reply.

"ARE YOU KIDDING ME?!? KENJI!!!"

As the Carnotaurus neared, Darius squeezed his eyes closed.

SCREECH!

Darius opened his eyes with a start. The sound wasn't the Carnotaurus chomping down on his legs. It was Kenji, standing there with a large tree branch, trying to pry the gate open!

The Carnotaurus charged, but Darius was still trapped. Just as the beast was about to close its mighty jaws on Darius's lower half, Kenji managed to lift the gate enough for Darius to wiggle through.

The branch snapped.

The gate slammed shut the moment the Carnotaurus reached it. The angry dinosaur rammed against the fence, snapping its jaws in pain and coming away with a large red gash on its face instead of a meal.

Realizing that they were, in fact, *still alive,* both boys grinned at each other and laughed.

"You got *nothing,* Toro!" Kenji taunted. Then he

looked at Darius and added, "Toro. Because of the horns."

Darius nodded. He got it. And then he asked, "Uh . . . what time are they supposed to get back from the lab?"

"Hey, guys!" Darius called out to the 6x4 as it pulled into camp.

He and Kenji emerged from behind the tank, grasping their shovels. Both boys were out of breath from sprinting back to camp.

As the kids and counselors stepped out of the car, they looked at Darius and Kenji and made absolutely terrible faces.

Guess we must not smell too good, Darius thought.

"Why are you two so out of breath?" Roxie asked.

"Just doing the job we were told," Darius said. Then, changing the subject, "How was the field trip?"

"Well, you know, Ben fell in love with a dinosaur," Yasmina said wryly. "And Superstar here got us booted from the lab."

"How'd poop patrol go?" Sammy asked.

"Awesome!" Kenji said. "You all should have seen how I owned—"

Thinking fast, Darius pretended to lose control of

the shovel in his hands and swung the handle right into Kenji's belly.

"This valuable experience!" Darius interjected, completing Kenji's sentence. "Learned a lot about ourselves, and, uh, yep!"

Kenji grabbed his stomach in pain.

"Well, then," Roxie said, not quite knowing what to say. "Hit the showers. And . . . maybe stay in there for a while."

The kids and counselors left. Kenji, still holding his stomach, glared at Darius, but Darius spoke first. "We can't tell *anyone* about Toro or we're *definitely* getting sent home."

Kenji moaned, rubbing his stomach. "I can't believe no one will know I saved your life."

"I'll know, Kenji," Darius said.

To Darius's surprise, Kenji's smile was genuine. "Thanks," Kenji replied. "So, we even now . . . Darius?"

Darius smiled at the sound of his name. "Yeah, we're even."

Night had fallen. Curfew had come and all the campers should have been inside.

But someone was walking through the jungle just outside camp. The loud SNAP of a twig threatened to draw the attention of a hungry dinosaur or a counselor. The mysterious figure waited for a moment, not moving, not even breathing. Then they proceeded into a clearing.

The late-night sounds of the jungle were soon interrupted by a mechanical whirring. A drone flew overhead and landed in the clearing.

The figure took a flash drive labeled JURASSIC WORLD—CLASSIFIED and placed it into a slot on the drone. They backed away just as the drone took off into the night sky.

"We thought it'd be fun," Darius said, his voice low and ominous. "We thought we'd be safe. But we didn't realize the horror waiting for us on the island . . . claws . . . teeth . . . screaming. So much screaming!"

A crack of thunder punctuated Darius's sentence, and Ben jumped up.

The kids had gathered around the firepit in the common room, as the night sky, full of clouds and storms, swirled above.

"The T. rex stalked closer, her jaws opened wide . . ."

FLASH!

Darius was blinded by Brooklynn's camera.

"For the vlog," Brooklynn said cheerfully. "Keep telling your little story!"

Annoyed, Darius continued. "The T. rex sta—"

"Dang!" Brooklynn said loudly, staring at her phone. "Out of space. Hold on." She started to delete some photos and videos. "I just don't wanna erase my selfie on Everest, ya know?"

Sammy looked very impressed.

"Maybe I should start over," Darius said, even more annoyed.

"NO!" Ben shouted. "In fact, you can just stop!"

Ben was behind Kenji, clutching onto his arms tightly.

"Dude, chill!" Kenji said. "He's not even telling the story right now, and *how is your grip this strong?*"

Darius took a deep breath and started again. "So the T. rex stalked—"

But he was distracted by Sammy, who was staring off into the distance.

"Shouldn't we call Yasmina over? I bet she'd love this story," Sammy said.

"Maybe she wants to be by herself," Brooklynn suggested.

"I think she's just shy and doesn't know how to make camp friends," Sammy said. She understood the demands that family—and unexpected circumstances—could put on a person. She could sense that Yasmina was a lot like her, and she was determined to get past the athlete's tough demeanor.

It started to rain, and the kids decided to call it a night. As they left, Brooklynn walked past Darius muttering, "Well, *that* was a waste of time."

"Park personnel are moving a group of dinosaurs to fresh grazing lands across the island," Roxie said, "and *we* get to ride along behind the herd."

"Are you kidding me?" Darius said, delighted. He looked at the gyrospheres like they were his birthday presents. "Dinosaur migration patterns are my jam!"

"You may wanna consider a new jam, bro," Kenji whispered. He walked over to a gyrosphere—a large ball-shaped see-through vehicle. Kenji knocked on it. "So, uh, you sure these things are waterproof? Looking pretty grim out here, and hair this awesome does *not* come easy."

"Your hair is gonna be fine, Kenji," Dave said. "The storm's already moved up the coast away from us."

"Cool," Kenji said. "Time to show these fools what a gyrosphere can do!"

Before Kenji could enter the gyrosphere, Roxie put a hand on his shoulder. "No way. Knowing you, you'll crash the thing, probably into a pack of Velociraptors. You're riding with Ben. As a passenger."

"Seriously?" Kenji protested.

"This is gonna be so sick," Yasmina said as she climbed into a gyrosphere. She sat in the driver's seat and took hold of the joystick controls.

"Right?" Sammy said, climbing in next to her.

"Yay," Yasmina said, clearly wanting to be by herself.

"Everyone! Seat belts at all times!" Dave called out.

Darius watched as the others got into their gyrospheres. Ben and Kenji were together, and Sammy and Yasmina were in another. There was only one gyrosphere left, and Brooklynn was sitting in it, on her phone. Darius frowned. He wished he could have his own gyrosphere.

"Darius, you need to ride with your fellow campers," Dave said. "Bond. Live the camp life!"

"Yeah, I tried last night, but not everyone was on board," Darius replied, looking at Brooklynn.

Dave leaned over and put his hand on Darius's shoulder. His smile was kind, but serious. "Buddy, you can't give up. You just need to get out there and show the other kids what you've got."

"All righty, campers!"

Darius could hear Dave's voice through the headset he was wearing. Brooklynn was next to him in the gyrosphere, and her eyes were glued to her phone.

"The headsets are for emergencies," Roxie said over the radio.

"Let the herding begin!" Dave cried.

He barely got the words out before the kids took off in their gyrospheres, leaving the counselors sitting in their 6x4.

Well, *most* of the kids took off. Ben was still sitting in the gyrosphere with Kenji, lurching forward, then hitting the brakes, then lurching forward, then brakes, and so on.

Kenji's face smacked into the Plexiglas a few times.

"Ha! I'm really getting the hang of this!" Ben said, proud of himself.

Kenji hit the glass again.

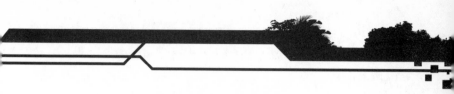

CHAPTER SIX

"**A**re you seeing this?" Darius said as he looked at a Brachiosaurus. "Whoaaaaaaaa!"

The kids were about a hundred feet behind the slow-moving herd of dinosaurs. Roxie and Dave were in the 6x4, following closely. Their transport jumped like it was hitting a speed bump every time one of the massive dinosaur's tree trunk–sized legs struck the ground.

The sky grew darker as Sammy peppered Yasmina with question after question, trying to draw her out.

"What's your favorite color?" Sammy asked. "Favorite food? Favorite color of food?"

"Orange, orange, and orange," Yasmina said, trying to end the conversation.

"Jokes!" Sammy said, nudging Yasmina. "I love jokes! Oooh, what do you and your friends do for fun?"

Unable to take it anymore, Yasmina yanked on the

joystick, causing the gyrosphere to lurch forward. It caught Sammy off guard, and she suddenly became quiet.

"How awesome is this?" Darius said. "We're, like, so close!"

Darius maneuvered their gyrosphere as close as he could to the dinosaurs, determined not to miss anything. Brooklynn, on the other hand, didn't seem to care at all. She was on her phone, looking at her latest video: "Ben Meets Bumpy!"

She had a frown on her face, though.

"'Used 2 b cool.' 'You made Jurassic World BORING,'" Brooklynn said, reading the comments on the video. "'Lame.' 'No one likes u NE more.'"

"Uh, hey, can you believe that an Ankylosaurus's tail is strong enough to shatter bone?" Darius said, changing the subject.

"Can you believe I don't care?" Brooklynn snapped. She looked at Darius, then softened.

"I'm sorry. I'm just . . . having one of those days. There's a lotta pressure when your whole life is about being popular. I'm not like you. I can't just tell a lame story and move on."

"Wasn't *that* lame," Darius said, a little hurt.

"Trust me, it was," Brooklynn said. "But you're not

even fazed! I just need people to . . . to like me."

Brooklynn stared at Darius. Then, sadly, she said, "You wouldn't understand."

CRACK!!!

Thunder echoed across the plain as the sky above continued to darken.

"I thought you said the storm rolled up the coast?" Roxie said, concerned.

"It must have rolled back down," Dave replied.

BOOM!!!

Another crash of thunder caused a Stegosaurus in front of the 6x4 to rear up. The creature swiped its tail, nearly taking out a nearby Ankylosaurus! The dinosaurs bellowed loudly.

Roxie hit the gas and drove in front of the kids in their gyrospheres, slamming the brakes. The gyrospheres came to a halt, as the herd of dinosaurs continued to move ahead without them.

Dave clapped his hands to get the kids' attention. They popped the hatches on their gyrospheres so they could hear him better.

"New plan!" Dave said. "The storm's getting worse, so . . . we're all going back to camp!"

Thunder rumbled threateningly.

"We're not gonna let a little rain stop us, are we?"

Darius said. "When else will we get the chance to ride alongside a herd of dinosaurs?"

Dave shook his head. "Sorry, can't risk it."

The radio in the 6x4 crackled, and Roxie picked up the receiver. "Hullo, hullo, Roxie here!" she said. There was only crackling in response. "Can you hear me? Anyone?"

"Okay, *new* new plan," Dave offered. "Storm's interfering with the radio, so Rox and I will drive ahead and tell the others we're pulling out. We'll be right back. Stay together and stay behind the herd."

Disappointed, Darius watched as Roxie and Dave drove off.

Lightning flashed, and thunder boomed, frightening a Sinoceratops. The dinosaur broke from the herd, and Darius watched, mouth agape, as the creature ran off in the opposite direction.

"That Sinoceratops is gonna get lost!" Darius said. "We need to go after her!"

"You heard Dave," Brooklynn said. "Let's just chill out and wait here."

"I've read *everything* about Sinoceratops behavior. We can get her!" Darius said.

Man, how can I convince her? Darius wondered. Then he thought of something.

"Your followers might really love a thrilling dino chase. . . ."

Brooklynn looked at Darius and smiled.

Darius sealed the gyrosphere, and Brooklynn raised her phone to start filming.

"Wait!" Sammy cried over the headset radio. "Are you guys going after her? I really don't think that's a good idea. I've seen cattle spook before, and—"

"Let's go!" Yasmina said, ignoring Sammy and pushing the joystick forward. The gyrosphere took off, following Darius and Brooklynn.

Then Kenji sealed the door to his and Ben's gyrosphere.

"Oh no," Ben said. "There's no way that I'm—"

"Great!" Kenji said. "*I'll* drive!"

The three gyrospheres were now racing off in pursuit of the frightened Sinoceratops. Darius was in the lead and had pulled up close behind the creature.

"Almost got you, girl!" Darius said.

The Sinoceratops veered. Only then did Darius see the enormous rock right in front of them! He pulled hard on the joystick, and the gyrosphere barely missed the boulder.

"Sorry," Darius said as Brooklynn nearly dropped her phone. "That was close."

Brooklynn reached into her mouth, removing a wad of gum she had been chewing. She placed it on the back of her phone, then stuck the phone to the dashboard of the gyrosphere.

"Voila!" she said proudly. "Instant phone mount."

"Great idea! And also, *ew.*"

"Just keep driving, Dino Nerd."

"Sure thing, Superstar."

The two grinned at each other as the gyrosphere raced forward.

"Come on, Darius! Get closer!" Brooklynn said.

"Someone flank her on the other side and we can lead her back to the herd!" Darius said over his headset.

"Wait, you'll scare her!" Sammy protested.

Then, out of nowhere, Kenji zoomed ahead, flanking the Sinoceratops opposite Darius and Brooklynn.

As Sammy predicted, the Sinoceratops panicked, making a loud noise.

But Darius's plan seemed to be working! The dinosaur was sandwiched between the two gyrospheres! Maybe they *could* lead it back to the herd!

"I'll cut her off. It'll be fine, Sammy!" Darius said. Then he moved his gyrosphere in front of the Sinoceratops. The creature reacted by making a U-turn and running away.

"Listen up, y'all," Sammy said. "We gotta get her before she goes and spooks the whole herd! Stay to the outside, or—"

Before she could finish, the two other gyrospheres zipped by in pursuit of the Sinoceratops.

"Relax," Yasmina said to Sammy. "Darius knows dinosaurs."

"We need to *gently* steer her away!" Sammy said.

"A Sinoceratops weighs two tons!" Darius replied over the headset. "She won't notice 'gentle'!"

"No, wait!" Sammy shouted, but it was too late. Darius had already moved his gyrosphere in front of the Sinoceratops. The dinosaur was totally spooked and knocked Darius and Brooklynn right into the herd!

"We've got multiple assets straying from the herd!" one of the park employees cried out.

"The kids!" Dave and Roxie said in unison. The counselors ran back to their 6x4, but before they could hop in—SMASH!—an Ankylosaurus knocked the vehicle over. Dave and Roxie had to dive out of the way to avoid being hit by their now airborne truck, which landed upside down with a loud crash.

The storm arrived, but it was nothing compared to the storm of dinosaurs that Darius and Brooklynn had stumbled into. They were weaving in and out of dinosaurs, doing their best to avoid becoming extinct themselves.

WHAP!

A Stegosaurus tail swatted the gyrosphere, knocking them right into Kenji and Ben. Yasmina twisted the joystick of her gyrosphere, managing to avoid both the collision *and* the Stegosaurus.

"Watch out!" Sammy shouted. "Stego, six o'clock! Tail! Tail! Tail!"

"Hang on!" Yasmina replied, as she skillfully maneuvered the gyrosphere away from each threat that Sammy called out.

The herd was now stampeding directly *toward* the kids.

Not knowing what else to do, the kids drove their gyrospheres off the plain and toward the thick jungle that surrounded them.

Maybe the dinosaurs won't follow . . . or they'll be confused and lay off, Darius thought.

"Low branch coming right at us!" Sammy shouted.

"I see it!" Yasmina shot back. "Let me concentrate!"

Then came a loud CRACK, but it wasn't a stampeding dinosaur. A bolt of lightning struck a huge tree in front of Yasmina's gyrosphere, causing it to fall right toward them! Yasmina managed to stop, but their gyrosphere was trapped in the fallen branches!

Meanwhile, Ben and Kenji's gyrosphere was zigzagging through the jungle as they continued to fight over the joystick.

"Left! Back to right! No, right!" Kenji said. "Back to left!"

"Fine, you drive!" Ben said, relenting. "Just get us out of here!"

"Finally," Kenji said, seizing the controls, only to smash into a tree.

"I think we lost them," Darius said as their gyrosphere emerged from the jungle. "Okay, think! Sinoceratops are fast on open ground, so we just need to corner her. Then we can get her back to the herd."

"Great!" Brooklynn said, climbing out of the gyrosphere. Looking into her phone, she said, "Here we go! Another Brooklynn exclusive! Keep watching, 'cause it's about to get real!"

"Brooklynn, wait!" Darius exclaimed. The hulking

Sinoceratops charged them.

"Too real! Too real!" Brooklynn announced, running back to the gyrosphere. She leaped in and buckled up right as the Sino slammed into the vehicle!

SLAM!

The Sinoceratops hit the gyrosphere again, its nose horn piercing the gyrosphere's Plexiglas shell. Then the creature lifted the gyrosphere off the ground and started to shake it back and forth, trying to dislodge its horn!

The kids were screaming as the Sino flung the gyrosphere off. In the process, the dinosaur's horn broke.

The gyrosphere crashed to the ground as the Sino raced into the jungle.

Darius and Brooklynn looked at each, realizing that they were still alive. They started to laugh.

Then they looked outside and saw the mud. The gyrosphere started to sink.

CHAPTER SEVEN

"**H**elp!" came the sound of Brooklynn's panicked voice over the static-filled headsets. "Can . . . ear us? We're stu . . . udhole . . . sinking! . . . elp!"

Snatching the headset's microphone, Sammy shouted, "Brooklynn? Brooklynn, can you hear me? Where are you?"

The only answer was more static.

"We gotta find them!" Sammy said to Yasmina. "Brooklynn! Darius!" Sammy called out.

"Guys!" Yasmina hollered. "Can you hear us?"

Having gotten clear of the fallen tree, Yasmina pushed hard to get the gyrosphere to go faster.

"Hello? Hello?" Yasmina said into her headset. "Can anybody hear me?"

"Still no sign of Ben and Kenji?" Sammy said, just as their gyrosphere almost ran into Ben and Kenji. The two boys had left their crashed gyrosphere and were on foot. They looked wet and miserable.

A minute later, all four kids were crammed into Sammy and Yasmina's gyrosphere, rumbling through the jungle. Suddenly, Kenji heard something from outside. It sounded like screaming—like Darius and Brooklynn!

"I hear them!" Kenji shouted. "They're over there!"

Mud poured in through the hole made by the Sino's horn. Time was running out. Darius threw his shoulder against the hatch, trying to force it open.

"It won't budge," Darius said. "The mud is jamming the doors!"

"Try driving out again!" Brooklynn suggested.

"We'll only sink deeper!" Darius said.

"Then YOU think of something, Mr. 'Let's Go Corner the Dinosaur'!"

Angry, Darius turned to glare at Brooklynn. The gyrosphere shifted and started to sink deeper and faster into the mud, which was closing in all around them. The mud was even covering the top of the gyrosphere.

"Brooklynn? Darius?"

It was Sammy!

"Hello? Sammy?" he shouted into the headset

"Do you read me?" Sammy said over the radio. "We're com . . . to . . . elp!"

The four kids had jumped out of the cramped gyrosphere and raced over to Darius and Brooklynn.

"Get us out of here!" Brooklynn shouted.

"Roxie? Dave? We've got a real emergency here!" Ben said into the radio.

Yasmina tried to grab hold of the muddy gyrosphere to pull it out but couldn't.

"It's too heavy!" Kenji said, straining.

"Ahhh!" Ben screamed. "It's gonna pull you under!"

Kenji realized that Ben was right! The suction of the mud pulling down the gyrosphere was taking him and Yasmina with it! They hobbled away from the vehicle.

"Uh, guys?" Ben said as lightning flashed overhead.

Between Ben and the lightning, everyone's attention was now on the Sinoceratops, who chose that particular moment to return. She pawed at the ground with a massive foot, ready to charge.

"I've got an idea," Sammy said. She moved toward

the Sinoceratops, arms out, drawing closer to the Sino. "Hey, I get it," she said gently. "It's hard to trust strangers. It's a scary world out there. But I'll trust you if you trust me."

Then Sammy placed a hand on the dinosaur, and the creature seemed to calm down almost immediately. Yasmina stared at Sammy in awe. The moment was so amazing, it almost made everyone forget that Darius and Brooklynn were sinking into a mudhole.

"Guys!" Darius shouted.

Sammy looked at Darius and Brooklynn, then at the Sinoceratops. "Hurry!" she ordered. Then she grabbed two vines and told the others her plan.

Kenji tied the vines together, making a rope. Yasmina grabbed one end and climbed a tree. She wrapped the vine around the tree for leverage and tossed it down to Darius. He reached up and grabbed the vine through the muddy hole in the gyrosphere. Pulling it in, he handed the vine to Brooklynn, who tied it around the dashboard.

Yasmina then gave the other end of the vine to Ben, and he and Kenji gently wrapped it around the Sinoceratops.

Sammy kept on soothing the dinosaur until Kenji flashed her the thumbs-up.

"Come on, girl," Sammy said to the Sino. "Easy.

That's it. Nice and slow. Let's go. You got this."

Then Sammy offered the Sinoceratops a branch of tasty leaves to eat. As the dinosaur munched on the foliage, Sammy guided her forward. In the process, the powerful Sinoceratops easily pulled Darius and Brooklynn from the mud!

The sky had opened up, and it was pouring rain harder than ever. Roxie and Dave found the kids and returned to camp. The kids were in the common room now as Sammy looked out the window and into the jungle, alone. At least, until Yasmina walked over to her.

"I . . . If everyone would've listened to you," Yasmina said softly. "If I had listened . . . we wouldn't have had any problems. I'm not so great at trusting . . . new people."

Then Yasmina took a deep breath and said, "My favorite color is black. My favorite food is pizza. . . ."

Suddenly, Sammy threw her arms around Yasmina. "I *knew* we were gonna be friends!" Sammy said.

"Not really a hugger," Yasmina said, pulling away from the other girl.

"You are now!"

Yasmina rolled her eyes, but then, giving in to the hug, she smiled.

Roxie and Dave had gone off to talk to the woman in charge of the Park. Herding dinosaurs and wrecking gyrospheres were definitely not supposed to be part of the camp experience. Before they left, both counselors had assured the campers that they were in *a lot* of trouble. This left Darius glum as he sat on a rock ledge that encircled the common room's dinosaur skeleton centerpiece. Brooklynn walked over to him.

"Hey, what's up?" she asked.

"I thought I knew everything about dinosaurs," Darius said quietly. "But all I did was mess up today. I just wanted . . ."

"People to like you?" Brooklynn said.

Darius looked at Brooklynn. "Yeah. I guess we have that in common."

The boy's face brightened.

"Well, tomorrow's a new day, and thanks to you, I've got a new video to show the Brooklanders. So I'm gonna go edit and post," she said, laughing. "Later, Dino Nerd."

Darius grinned despite himself.

Back in the girls' room, Brooklynn settled in on her bunk, looking at her phone. She was replaying the video she had just shot. There she was with Darius in the gyrosphere, rocking back and forth, zigzagging through a sea of dinosaurs.

Everything was there, including the uncomfortable "after" moment when Dave and Roxie arrived and the kids were getting chewed out. Brooklynn watched as she saw everyone gathering around, except . . . except for Sammy.

She noticed that Sammy was hanging in the background, near the Sinoceratops. She was scraping something against the Sino's cheek. Then she put the sample in a tiny vial and slipped it into her pocket before rejoining the group.

"What the . . . ?" Brooklynn said, as she paused on the image of Sammy. She was so lost in the video that Brooklynn hadn't noticed Sammy standing in the doorway.

The next morning, Darius walked into the common room. His enthusiasm had returned after a good night's rest. "What up, Camp Cretaceous? WOO-HOO!" he hollered.

His attempt at cheer was met with dead silence. Sammy and Yasmina just stared at him, then looked back at each other and Yasmina's sketchbook. Ben took a loud sip from a juice box. Kenji leaned back in his chair, shaking his head.

"Not in a 'woo-hoo' mood this morning, Darius," Kenji said. "Not after yesterday. Trekking through a rainstorm will do that."

Taking another loud sip, Ben said, "We only had to walk because *you* crashed our gyrosphere."

"Today's kayak day!" Darius said, trying again. "Who doesn't wanna paddle alongside dinosaurs? *Real* dinosaurs! It's going to be awesome . . . right?"

Still no reaction. Then Darius noticed something was amiss.

"Wait . . . where are Dave and Roxie?" he asked.

"The babysitters took off early and left *this*," Kenji said. He handed a children's menu from a Jurassic World restaurant to Darius.

Darius flipped it over and read, " 'We have to go talk to our boss. Stay inside until we return—draw, bond, whatever. The radio's set for Channel Six in case you need us. Stay inside, *stay inside*, do *not* leave (Kenji, looking at you). Sorry for the kids' menus. They're all Dave had.' "

Then the door swung open, and Brooklynn entered. Sammy looked at her, not saying anything.

"What's new on the internet, Superstar?" Yasmina said.

"I wouldn't know," Brooklynn said tersely. "Because when I went to get my phone from its charger, it *wasn't there.* Someone *stole* my phone!"

Brooklynn paused, waiting for someone to confess. After a tense moment of silence, Yasmina said, "Brooklynn . . . who *hasn't* had your phone?"

"I needed to check the weather last night because I was scared of, you know, another near-death experience today," Ben confessed.

"Dr. Sattler posted a new column about microfossils yesterday," Darius added sheepishly.

"The lighting this morning was too good to miss the selfie-op," Kenji added. "But I haven't used it since then and definitely put it back. I swear!"

"I . . . haven't seen it, either," Sammy said.

Brooklynn's eyes narrowed. "Really . . ."

"Hey, hey, it's okay!" Darius said. "Since we're not kayaking till later, we'll have plenty of time to look for the phone."

"Oh, I think I know *exactly* where to look," Brooklynn said. "I also think that whoever took the phone might be trying to hide some of the things that are on it. What do you think, Sammy?"

"Uh, what?" Sammy said unconvincingly.

Yasmina stepped in between the two girls. "What is your deal? Sammy said she didn't touch it. Ever think you might have just lost the stupid thing?"

Brooklynn glared at Yasmina, then headed for the door. "Well, then. Let's check her bags!"

"You do *not* get to go through anyone's stuff," Yasmina said, stopping her.

"Brooklynn, I did not—" Sammy stuttered.

Then Darius jumped in front of the door, blocking Brooklynn's exit. "Brooklynn, guys, come on! We can't be this upset over phones. Let's make the most of this incredible opportunity! This is Jurassic World! It's . . . it's . . ."

But a loud ROAR cut Darius off before he could finish.

"What was that?" Brooklynn asked.

"Where's it coming from?" Sammy said.

"Can't see anything from here. The trees are blocking everything," Yasmina said, frustrated.

"Maybe they're moving a new dino from the lab to another enclosure?" Darius offered. "We could probably see it from the Observation Tower!"

Sammy grabbed Darius's hand. "Wow, that's a great idea, Darius! What are we waiting for?"

"Hey, we're not done talking about this yet," Brooklynn said, shooting Sammy a harsh look. But Sammy had already pulled Darius out of the common room. Brooklynn followed, then Kenji, and finally, a reluctant Ben.

If they'd only stayed for a few seconds longer, they would have heard the announcement over the radio: *"Asset out of containment. Repeat: Asset out of containment. Stay indoors!"*

Darius and the others had made it to the Observation Tower and raced up the stairs. When they reached the top, they were all out of breath, except for Yasmina. The snapping of tree branches could be heard, and then there was a Brachiosaurus walking alongside the jungle.

"It's just a Brachiosaurus," Yasmina said, relieved.

"Mystery solved," Ben said. "Guess we should head back now!"

"But that doesn't make any sense," Darius said, puzzled. "Brachiosauruses don't *roar*."

Leaning over the edge of the Tower, the kids noticed two workers running out of the jungle. They seemed to be in a panic and started to shout at the kids—but the group was too high up to hear them.

"What are they saying?" Darius asked.

"They look mad," Ben said.

Kenji waved at the worker. "You're gonna have to speak up!"

A worker screamed at the kids, but they still couldn't hear.

Suddenly, the Brachiosaurus lurched, crashing into a stand of trees as she howled in pain. Something huge and invisible seemed to be dragging her down. The thing pulled the Brachiosaurus into the jungle until she could be seen no more.

CHAPTER EIGHT

The trees where the Brachiosaurus had disappeared began to sway. Something huge and unseen was thundering through the jungle, coming their way. The kids ran to the edge to get a better look.

At that moment, an enormous dinosaur appeared as if out of thin air. The kids didn't know it, but this was the Indominus rex! The creature had been camouflaged until a second ago. Now she lunged forward, racing through the trees and man-made structures with terrifying abandon.

The workers who had tried to warn Darius and the kids started to run, but by then, it was already far too late. The Indominus rex crushed one worker beneath an enormous foot. Then she made a grab for another park employee with her claws.

The kids screamed as the Indominus rex roared and thrashed its tail.

"What. Is. *That?*" Yasmina said.

"Dr. Wu's lab," Brooklynn said. "There was a dinosaur. Indom—"

"Indominus rex," Sammy said in a frightened whisper.

"How do *you* know that name?" Brooklynn asked suspiciously.

"We need to leave," Sammy said. "Now, now, now!"

Looking down at the Indominus rex, the kids were horrified to see the great dinosaur staring up at them.

"It sees us!" Ben shouted.

The Indominus rex ran toward the Tower at a full sprint. With her awful claws, she scratched at the sides of the Tower as if she was going to climb it. The claws were tearing away chunks of the Tower's foundation, weakening it, and the building began to sway.

Ben nearly went over the side as the Indominus slammed into the Tower again.

Sammy *did* go over. With incredible speed, Yasmina thrust her hand over the side of the Tower, catching her.

"Hold on!" Darius shouted. He and Kenji helped Yasmina pull Sammy back.

The Tower leaned, and the kids tumbled. Thinking as one, the group headed for the zip line.

Kenji snapped a harness on Ben, tight as it would go on the slender boy.

Below, the Indominus continued to attack the Tower, and the structure leaned even more.

Ben tried to stay on the Tower, but Kenji pushed him off the edge. Ben screamed the entire way down the zip line.

Right behind him were Sammy, Kenji, and Brooklynn.

Then it was Darius's and Yasmina's turn to go. As they slid down the zip line, Darius saw the Indominus rex finally topple the Tower. No one had yet reached the end of the zip line, however. As the supports crumbled, the zip line went slack.

Darius and his friends fell into the jungle below.

The tree branches must have slowed our fall, Darius thought, rubbing his head. He'd landed on the ground only moments ago.

Looking around, he saw that everyone was accounted for. Then the ground beneath their feet rumbled.

"It's coming," Ben said worriedly.

"It could be anywhere," Yasmina gasped.

"The Observation Tower was that way?"

Brooklynn wondered in a daze, spinning around. "Or was it that way?"

Sammy looked at Brooklynn. "Okay, I'm sorry, but I . . ."

Giving up trying to explain, she reached into her pocket and pulled out Brooklynn's phone. Or rather, what remained of it. The phone had been smashed in the fall. Sammy quickly hid the broken phone pieces.

"Where is . . ." Darius said. He felt for his Raptor necklace, the one his dad had given him. It wasn't there! Had it fallen off? "No, no, my necklace!"

Then he remembered. "I left it in my bunk!"

"We've got slightly bigger problems," Kenji said as the Indominus roared and the ground shook.

The kids were off and running, ducking under tree branches as they raced through the jungle—away from the Indominus rex!

"Everything will be fine when we get back to camp," Darius said. He hoped.

They kept on running, and no one looked back, not even for a second.

They arrived at the Camp Cretaceous base, only to find that the compound had already been ravaged by the Indominus rex.

Deep, clawed footprints could be seen all over

the campgrounds. The common room had crashed to the ground, and several of the rope bridges that connected the various tree houses together had been ripped down. The elevator had been smashed, too.

There would be no way to get up to the bunks.

Or my necklace, Darius thought.

The Indominus rex roared again, but Darius could tell that the roar was receding—the dinosaur was moving in the opposite direction from camp.

"Dave, Roxie . . . they must have all gotten away," Sammy said hopefully.

"We're on our own," Yasmina said matter-of-factly.

In that moment, a furious Brooklynn turned to face Sammy. "Give. Me. My. Phone!" she ordered.

"Wha—" Sammy said.

"I don't care about you sneaking into Dr. Wu's lab, I don't care about whatever you did with the skin samples you took from the Sinoceratops," Brooklynn said rapidly.

"What skin samples?" Yasmina asked.

"What do you mean, Dr. Wu's lab?" Kenji said.

"I don't even care that you stole it now. All I want to do is call for help. Where is it?" Brooklynn demanded.

Sammy touched her pocket—the one that she knew contained what was left of Brooklynn's phone. But instead of telling the truth, she said, "I . . . I don't know what you're talking about! Skin samples? Sneaking into labs? You made up some crazy thing in your own dang head!"

Yasmina got between them. "Hey, back off," she said. "Not everything revolves around you and your phone! It isn't Sammy's fault you lost it!"

"Would you guys please keep it down?" Ben said. "There's a big—"

"A big scary dinosaur?" Kenji said, shutting him down. "Of *course* there's a big scary dinosaur! There's *always* a big scary dinosaur!"

"And you're always a big-mouthed jerk!" Ben countered.

Everyone was now arguing. Darius watched them and backed away slowly. He was focused on the bunks in the tree above. The arguing was growing louder now and becoming particularly vicious. Everyone was saying mean things about everyone else.

Until finally Ben shouted, "NO ONE IS GETTING OUT OF HERE!"

Suddenly, everyone stopped fighting.

"We just saw people get *eaten*!" Ben continued. "We're alone, we're defenseless . . . we're dead."

Darius looked at his friends, who seemed to be giving up entirely. He thought about his necklace. The one his dad had given him. Suddenly, he missed his dad more than ever. But his friends were here. Right now. And they needed his help.

"We're not giving up!" Darius said loudly. "I get it. It's scary. This isn't how this was supposed to be.

But things don't always go our way. Life is messy, and sometimes things fall apart. But that's okay. Because when that happens, we pick up the pieces and keep going. And we *never* give up."

"What are we supposed to do?" Yasmina asked.

"Get south to the Park. Get help. And the only way we'll make it is if we do it together. We're a team or we're nothing at all."

The enclosure fence had held this long at least. That was, until the Carnotaurus came along. He took a look and growled.

Something else was there, too.

On the other side of the fence, the Indominus rex thundered into view. The two carnivores looked at each other, unsure what to do next.

Then the Indominus roared and brought its claws down on the fence.

I know where we are! Darius suddenly thought. "The Carnotaurus. We're by Toro's paddock!"

Darius pushed aside some ferns. Behind the foliage, there was a large cable fence. Except it wasn't exactly a whole fence. The cables had been ripped down, leaving a huge opening.

"I remember this fence!" Darius said, finally seeing the hole. "The broken . . . ripped-down . . . fence."

Darius shot Kenji a worried glance.

"That means Toro is out here," Ben said, breathing heavily. "With us!"

"Now we have to deal with Indominus *and* Toro," Darius said. Then he swiveled to look at Ben. "Hold up. How do *you* know about Toro?"

"We all know," Yasmina said. "Kenji told us, like, the day after it happened."

"In my defense, me saving you was super cool," Kenji said. Darius glared at him.

"We know this enclosure is due north of the Main Park," Darius said, thinking out loud. Then he pointed in the opposite direction. "So if we keep going *that* way, we'll hit the Visitor Center. We're sure to find Dave and Roxie or someone else there in charge."

"Yes, exactly what I was thinking," Kenji said. "As a leader, which I am. Follow me!"

The kids had only been gone for about a half a minute when the trees rustled and an enormous foot stepped out. The Indominus rex had been watching. Now she was following them, too.

CHAPTER NINE

"**Y**az?" Sammy said quietly. "There's something I—"

But before she could confess to Yasmina, she saw the other girl had frozen in her tracks, along with the other kids.

Right in front of them was a shattered gyrosphere. There were giant footprints surrounding the gyrosphere, and clawed, torn-up earth. There were even remains of an unfortunate Ankylosaurus.

"The Indominus rex was here," Brooklynn said.

The plants behind them rustled. Something leaped at them! The kids screamed, jumping back. The dinosaur moved back, too. It was moaning loudly, but it wasn't the Indominus rex.

"Bumpy!" Ben exclaimed.

The dinosaur, now much bigger than the last time they had seen her, mewed at the sight of Ben. Bumpy remembered him! Ben gave Bumpy a big hug.

"As fun as this reunion is, shouldn't we keep moving south?" Kenji said.

Brooklynn shook her head. "I'm not spending another hour walking through the jungle *hoping* that we don't run into that Indominus. We need a new plan."

"Okay . . . so, uh . . . we need to find somewhere safe close by," Darius said, thinking on his feet. "Isn't Dr. Wu's field genetics lab near here? You guys went on the tour. Does this area look familiar?"

Sammy looked around, then pointed in a different direction. "Yeah! Yeah, I think it might be over that way!"

"Great!" Darius said with a deep sigh. "That's where we should go. There's bound to be an adult there who can help. . . . Right?"

No one said anything. Not because they didn't have anything to say. But because a dinosaur answered first with a terrifying roar.

The Indominus rex was nearby!

Everyone was flat-out sprinting toward the genetics lab. Everyone except . . .

"Wait! Guys! Where's Ben?" Darius called out.

He squinted and saw that Ben . . . and Bumpy were way, way behind.

"We don't have time for this," Yasmina said. "There are dinosaurs eating people out here, and Bumpy can't keep up!"

Frustrated, Ben threw up his arms. "Then, then . . ." He stopped talking as he saw something in the distance. "We'll put her in the van!"

"What van?" Sammy asked.

They turned around as Ben pointed at a van ahead of them.

"It's an ACU transport!" Kenji said, pulling open the van door. "Asset Containment Unit. Got the tour of their HQ—super hard-core dino-trapping security dudes."

"Then where are they?" Darius said, looking around.

"Is that a tablet?" Brooklynn said as she shoved Kenji aside and jumped into the passenger seat. There was an ACU tablet sitting on it, and Brooklynn wasted no time in grabbing it and turning it on, swiping her finger on the screen.

Sammy looked in and found a radio that had been left on the backseat. She picked it up, fiddled with a knob, and turned it to Channel Six. "Dave, Roxie! Can y'all hear us?"

But there was only static on the radio.

Before she could try again, there was a loud BEEP! The sound came from the ACU tablet. The kids gathered around Brooklynn as she swiped the screen.

"There's a map program running with little moving dots on it," she said.

"They chip all the dinosaurs electronically to track them, see?" Darius said, pointing at the screen. "There's us, and there's—"

Darius tapped one of the dots that was far from them on the map. An ID popped up that said BRACHIOSAURUS.

"Here's the Brachiosaurus Grove on the map. So why are the Brachiosauruses way over there?" Darius said.

Then they heard—and felt—the sound of heavy feet on ground. In the distance, trees were shaking, branches fluttering.

Bumpy pawed at Ben, mewing impatiently.

"Easy girl," Ben said. "Guys, something's coming this way...."

"That's weird," Brooklynn said, staring at the tablet. "Whatever that is, it isn't showing up on the tablet."

"What kind of dinosaur wouldn't have a transponder?" Darius asked.

"I am *not* in the mood to find out!" Kenji replied, terrified.

Then came a bone-chilling ROAR again.

"Doesn't anyone know how to drive a van?" Darius asked. The kids were now scrunched into the backseat.

"No," Sammy said. "But we drove gyrospheres, right? It can't be that different!"

"I don't even have my learner's permit!" Ben said.

"I do!" Kenji boasted as he jumped into the driver's seat. Gripping the steering wheel, Kenji hit the accelerator, and the van took off!

In reverse!

The Indominus rex burst through the trees and ran right for them!

Kenji hit the brakes, put the car in drive, and gunned the engine. The van pulled ahead of the Indominus, but the dinosaur was quick.

"It's gainin'! Go faster!" Sammy said, thumping her hand against the back of Kenji's seat. Bumpy squealed.

The Indominus was almost on top of them!

"TURN!!!" Brooklynn screamed.

Kenji yanked the wheel to the right. The van spun around and took off in the opposite direction. The angry Indominus slowed down briefly as it changed direction.

"She's coming back!" Darius screamed.

Suddenly, the Indominus crashed through the trees to their right and pulled up alongside the van!

Yasmina reached over the seat, grabbed the steering wheel, and turned the van left. They swerved away from the Indominus!

And over the edge of a really, really steep hill!

The van went airborne, and when its wheels hit the ground, the van kept on building up speed, going faster and faster down the hill. They crashed through trees, branches hitting the windshield.

The bottom of the hill was approaching rapidly as Yasmina reached forward again and pulled hard on the emergency brake. The van came to a complete stop . . . right in front of the genetics lab.

"We are *so* happy we found you," Darius said. He was talking to a guy named Eddie, a lab tech who had been hiding in the genetics lab. The kids noticed that Eddie wore a party hat on his head and that the room had been decorated with a few streamers that hung from the ceiling. There was also a birthday cake. And because no one had eaten in, like, forever, the kids each had a slice.

"Things are crazy!" Darius continued. "There's a

giant camouflaged dinosaur out there! Also regular dinosaurs! We've been hoping to find someone to—"

"You're sure you closed the door behind you, right?" Eddie said, cutting him off.

"Uh, I think so."

Eddie spun around. "You think or you know?"

Eddie looked down the hall, staring at a door. Darius noticed. So did Kenji.

Then Brooklynn started smacking the buttons on a phone. "There's no dial tone!"

"The land lines are down," Eddie said, looking distracted. "So is the radio, and cellphone service keeps cutting out."

"But the Park obviously has a plan," Darius said. "So . . . what's the plan?"

Eddie laughed. "Do you not get it? We're *doomed.* No one is coming to help!"

Kenji asked, "But what about Dr. Wu or—"

"*Wu?* Who do you think is to blame?" Eddie yelled. "Wu got greedy, and instead of dinosaurs, he built monsters! Masrani, Dearing, they're all *clueless* about what's really going on here. Jurassic World isn't a park. It's a powder keg, and it is detonating all around us!"

Then Eddie collapsed into a chair and scowled at the kids.

"No, you *have* to know what to do," Darius said. "We drove all the way here 'cause—"

Eddie reached up and grabbed Darius by his shirt. "Whoa, drove? You have a vehicle?"

Then Eddie pushed Darius aside and ran out of the lab.

"Guys?" Kenji said sheepishly. "I, uh, left the keys in the van."

The kids ran after Eddie.

Eddie was already halfway to the van when the kids emerged from the lab.

"Stop!" Darius shouted. "What are you doing?"

Eddie kept on running, moving way ahead. "Getting out of here alive!" he yelled over his shoulder.

Yasmina took off in a sprint. If anybody could overtake Eddie, it was her.

But Bumpy squealed and stopped short in front of Yasmina. She tripped, falling down. Shooting Bumpy and Ben an angry look, she got up and started running after Eddie again.

It was too late, though. Eddie had reached the van and was already behind the wheel. He started the engine and took off.

The kids were chasing after the van as it raced down a jungle road.

Yasmina turned on the speed, her legs and arms pumping as she sprinted toward the van. She was getting closer! The van was almost in reach. She stretched out a hand, about to touch it—

ROOOOOOOAAAAAAAARRRRRR!

Suddenly, the Indominus rex burst out of the trees and slammed into the van!

CHAPTER TEN

Eddie screamed and Yasmina dove for the ground hard as the fearsome dinosaur kicked the van with a clawed foot. The vehicle spun around in a circle. As soon as it came to a stop, Eddie jumped from it and ran. Sensing fear and an easy kill, the Indominus charged after him.

Deciding quickly that it was better to be anywhere the Indominus wasn't, the kids and Bumpy took off in the opposite direction, running into the jungle.

As they fled, they could hear the horrible growls and roars of the Indominus. Eddie's screams filled their ears.

They kept on running until they came to a huge cable fence. If they could get past it, they could keep running through the jungle. But how could they do that? It was too high!

"Perfect," Kenji said with a heavy dose of sarcasm. "The Park's only intact fence!"

The kids hugged the side of a large tree as they looked around. There were piles of old, rusted metal barrels and a large metal container that had been used a long time ago.

There was another loud roar from the Indominus. Eddie's screams could no longer be heard.

The kids looked toward the abandoned van and saw the Indominus raise her head. Hanging from one of its teeth was Eddie's birthday hat. It fell to the ground, and the Indominus stepped on it.

The dinosaur came closer to the kids, moving slowly. Bumpy got between them and started braying.

"Shhhhh!" Ben said, trying to keep her quiet.

What are we gonna do? Darius thought. He looked around and saw boulders, trees, the metal barrels . . . the metal barrels.

Darius shook his head and put a finger to his lips, indicating for everyone to be quiet. Ben covered Bumpy's mouth. Darius motioned for them to follow. They looked scared, but he smiled.

The kids hid behind the metal barrels as the Indominus rex lumbered their way. Darius had gambled everything on the world's most dangerous game of hide-and-seek. And he was praying that they were lucky enough to win . . . and live.

The massive dinosaur cocked its head, listening, trying to find its prey.

Darius peeked out from behind the barrel to see where the Indominus might be. She was right in front of him.

The dinosaur roared. Darius ducked back and bolted.

The Indominus whipped around the corner, trying to catch Darius, but he was no longer there. The kids had moved on, slipping around the side of the shipping container.

But Ben and Kenji were missing! Darius looked around, trying to spot any sign of them. He saw them at last, stuck behind one of the big boulders. *Gotta help 'em get over here,* Darius thought. Then he had an idea. Darius picked up a rock, ran to the opposite end of the shipping container, and threw it.

The rock landed and made enough noise to lure the Indominus away. Ben and Kenji ran!

Just then, Brooklynn dropped the tablet. It landed with a clatter. The Indominus jerked its head. The dinosaur was now heading right for them! Brooklynn was sure this was the end, until Sammy yanked her behind a tree.

The Indominus was drawing closer . . . and closer . . . her fangs only inches away from them. The Indominus whipped its head around and headed in the direction of a nearby sound. It distracted the

Indominus just long enough for the kids to make a break.

The two girls sprinted across the way to join the others behind a pile of metal barrels.

The van was now in sight. The kids ran and piled inside. Yasmina started it up. She went slowly at first to keep the engine quiet, but as soon as she thought they were out of the carnivore's earshot, she hit the gas. The Indominus got smaller and smaller in the rearview mirror every second as the van raced away.

"We're getting out of here!" Brooklynn said. She looked at Sammy and smiled.

"We did it, camp family!" Sammy said brightly. She moved to high-five Brooklynn as the van hit a bump—and the broken pieces of Brooklynn's phone spilled out of her pocket!

"My phone!" Brooklynn said. "I *knew* it!"

Yasmina looked at Sammy in disbelief. "Sammy?"

She should have been looking at the road, not at Sammy. Because Yasmina was distracted just long enough for the van to crash into a creek bed.

"Is everyone . . ." Yasmina started to say, and then she laughed bitterly.

She got out of the van and slammed the door shut behind her.

"Yaz, wait, wait!" Sammy said, following her out of the van. Yasmina stood there with her back to the group as they climbed out of the van. Sammy approached and noticed that Yasmina's fists were clenched.

"Yasmina—" Sammy said.

"We're *not* okay!" Yasmina said. "We're in the middle of a jungle with a monster dinosaur out there. And *you*. You . . ."

Suddenly, Brooklynn was there, laying into Sammy. "Destroyed our only way to get help and lied about it! I told you guys!"

"So you *did* take Brooklynn's phone," Darius said, stunned. "Why? What were you doing?"

"Probably trying to erase my video of her taking those samples from the Sinoceratops," Brooklynn said. Then she gasped. "And you knew about the Indominus rex because you were snooping around Dr. Wu's office when I ran into you!"

"Hold up, what were *you* doing in Dr. Wu's office, Brooklynn?" Darius asked.

"I—it doesn't matter," she said. "I didn't break our only way to call for help and then lie about it! This is not my fault! This is *her* fault! She—"

"I'm here to spy!" Sammy blurted. All eyes were on her. "For a company called Mantah Corp."

Darius wrinkled his brow. "Mantah Corp? They're a bioengineering company. Big rivals with Masrani and Biosyn. They also tried to make dinosaurs, but Wu beat them to it."

"You doomed us all for some lousy company?" Ben croaked.

"Our ranch was in trouble, so my folks had to borrow a lot of money from some . . . shady people," Sammy explained. "We didn't know they were fronting for Mantah Corp. They said we'd lose everything unless I spied for them. Used the 'behind-the-scenes access' I'd get at camp to gather info from Wu's lab, and DNA from dinos, and whatever else they needed. But then Brooklynn caught on and I got scared, and then . . . everything went wrong."

Sammy slumped, defeated. Then she looked at Yasmina. "This is so the last thing I wanted to happen."

"To be next to a broken van on killer-dinosaur island?" Yasmina said sarcastically. "Hey, me too. What are the odds?"

"Yaz, I—"

"Was it all a lie?" Yasmina said, getting in Sammy's face. "Wanting to be friends? Pretending you cared about . . . ? You just needed someone to hide what you were doing."

Sammy started to speak, but the words wouldn't come. Then she started to cry.

"I'm such an idiot," Yasmina said.

"You're wrong. I just didn't know how to say it—how to explain it to you! Just because I spied doesn't change who I am or how I feel or—"

Sammy put a hand on Yasmina's shoulder. Yasmina pushed her away.

"Don't touch me!" she shouted. "Go away, Sammy."

"Not now, Bumpy," Yasmina said. She was in no mood for company, even if it was in the form of a ridiculously cute dinosaur. Bumpy mewed and rubbed her head against Yasmina's hand, but Yasmina gently shooed her away.

The Ankylosaurus mewed again and butted up against Ben. He patted her on the head as she became more insistent, nudging Ben harder. "Bumpy, what are you . . . ?" Ben started to say.

Suddenly, the kids became quiet, as the THUMP, THUMP, THUMP of heavy footsteps could be heard. The ground vibrated, and Yasmina and Ben exchanged looks—so *that's* why Bumpy was trying to get their attention.

From out of the trees, the Indominus rex appeared, roaring in anger. But she wasn't after the kids!

Looking up, they noticed a helicopter! The Indominus leaned forward, running back into the forest, chasing the helicopter.

Jurassic World is a lush island resort where people can visit real live dinosaurs. Six lucky kids have been picked to try out the park's new camp—CAMP CRETACEOUS!

CAMP CRETACEOUS

DARIUS is a dino-nerd extraordinaire. He was the first to beat the Jurassic World video game, so he gets to go to Camp Cretaceous. He can't wait to meet his campmates . . . and the dinosaurs!

An adorable Ankylosaurus hatches from an egg. She hatched early, so the bumps on her head are uneven. Dr. Wu doesn't think she is good enough for the park . . .

. . . but the kids love her. One of the campers, Ben, names the little dinosaur **BUMPY**.

CAMP CRETACE

Unfortunately, not all the dinosaurs are as cute as Bumpy. Darius and the other campers get into a lot of trouble with a Carnotaurus they name **TORO**.

Smart pack hunters that are armed with a sharp slashing claw on each foot, Velociraptors are both cunning and dangerous!

The fiercest Velociraptor is **BLUE**, but she is also the smartest and most used to humans. But how will she react to the campers when they enter her territory?

They ran through the jungle, skidding to a halt at the edge of a cliff. In the distance, they could see the Aviary—where the flying dinosaurs were kept. The helicopter was flying overhead, and the Indominus roared. Sure enough, the helicopter got closer to the Indominus and started to fire.

"Yeah, kick its butt, Masrani! Woo-hoo!" Kenji cried, recognizing the park owner's call sign stenciled on the chopper. "We're saved! Yeah, baby! I told you, they've got it totally under con—"

The helicopter crashed into the Aviary, creating a massive hole in the glass structure. An explosion followed, shattering most of the glass. Pteranodons flew out of the Aviary and over the main tourist area of the Park. Soon, screams could be heard from miles away.

While the others looked on in horror, Brooklynn turned to the tablet. Her fingers danced across the screen as she searched for something.

"The Main Park is over that ridge," Kenji said, pointing as his finger shook.

Brooklynn showed everyone the screen. "There's some kind of path here that might—"

"The Kayak River!" Kenji exclaimed. "The entrance is near here. It goes underground, beneath the ridge! If we follow it, it'll take us right to the Main Park!"

"Jurassic World River Adventurers!"

Ben nearly jumped out of his skin at the voice that came over the loudspeakers.

"Prepare yourselves for the wonder of the underground river!" It was just the pre-recorded voice of a park announcer!

"Guys, we can still make it to the Park. Everyone, grab a kayak!" Darius said, relieved.

The park announcer went over the various safety procedures as Darius and his friends grabbed life jackets and paddles. The kids broke up into groups, with Brooklynn and Kenji in one kayak. Darius was going to go with Ben and Bumpy, but Yasmina grabbed them instead. She didn't want to go with Sammy.

Sammy, looking sad, approached Darius. "Come on, Sammy, let's get out of here," he said. She went with him and jumped into his kayak.

If only they had noticed the looming shadow that flitted around the cavern . . .

CHAPTER ELEVEN

Darius looked up at the incredible bioluminescent cavern through which they paddled. *It's like another world!* he thought.

The cavern was bathed in colorful lights that danced along the rocky formations, playing off the water. At times, the kids were barely even paddling. They watched as the gentle Parasaurolophuses glowed in vivid blues and greens, a result of the dinosaurs grazing on the abundant bioluminescent plants growing throughout the cave.

Brooklynn broke the silence. "We're here because of her!" She was still stewing about her phone and Sammy.

"Or maybe something else would have happened and we would still be stuck here," Kenji offered. Brooklynn blinked and stared at Kenji. She hadn't thought of that.

"Look, I . . . I know you're mad at Sammy," Kenji

said. "But getting mad doesn't get us out of here. It just . . . makes more people mad, you know? Put yourself in her shoes. At this point, is there anything you could say that would make Sammy feel worse than she already does?"

Brooklynn was quiet. She glanced at Sammy sitting in Darius's kayak, paddling silently.

"Just ask," Sammy said lifelessly.

"It's just that you talk so much about your ranch and your family," Darius began. "But your family *sent* you here. To break the law."

"They didn't send me. They said no to Mantah Corp. They said they'd rather lose everything than use me like that."

Darius looked at Sammy, surprised.

"I was the one who contacted the Mantah Corp agent. I agreed to come here. My family . . . they didn't even know what I was planning until I was already on the ferry. Smashing the phone was an accident, but . . . Brooklynn's right. This is all my fault."

"I still don't see why . . ."

Sammy turned to face Darius and stared him straight in the eye. "If your family was in trouble, wouldn't you do anything in your power to save them?"

The group took a momentary break and stopped paddling. But something was wrong.

Darius flinched as Sammy grabbed his arm, nails digging into his skin. "If we stopped paddling," she said, "why are we still movin' forward?"

Looking down into the river, Darius could just see that the kayak was being pulled ahead. The sound of rushing water could be heard in the distance. Glancing up, Darius thought he could make out some kind of opening ahead. It looked like there had once been a grate that covered the opening.

Something had ripped it apart.

"Paddle!" Darius cried out. "There's a current pulling us into a different tunn—"

But it was already too late. The current was far too strong and pulled the kayaks down into the dark tunnel.

When the kayaks emerged, it took Darius a second to realize they had emerged into daylight once again! Well, dusk, anyway.

The water was calm as the three kayaks drifted away from each other.

"We're okay!" Ben shouted.

Sammy laughed. They all felt a rush of relief that

the current had not led them into a more dangerous situation . . . until . . .

Kenji gasped. "Guys—we're in the Jurassic World Lagoon," he said. "And so is the Mosasaurus!"

Darius gulped as just beneath the surface of the water, the massive shadow of *the* largest creature at Jurassic World swam below them.

"It's circling," Brooklynn said, scared. "Testing us. It's acting like a shark. We're intruders in its domain, so it's investigating us . . . before it gets confident and it decides to . . ."

"This is bad," Brooklynn concluded.

"We have to get out . . . now!" Kenji concurred.

Darius looked around to see what their escape options might be. The walls that surrounded the lagoon were way too high to climb. Turning his head, he saw the empty spectator stands on the other side of the wall. There was a ladder on the rail in front of the stands.

The walls may be out, Darius thought. *But the ladder . . .*

Suddenly, the kayaks began to bob up and down in the water, as the Mosasaurus's tail fin breeched the water's surface. The water was roiling and the kayaks along with it.

"Paddle!" Darius shouted. "Go, go!"

He pointed toward the ladder, and the kids paddled with all the strength they could muster.

It was hard to tell what was making the biggest waves in the lagoon—the Mosasaurus or the furious paddling of six kids.

Kenji and Brooklynn had reached the ladder and were motioning for the others to join them.

But Darius and Sammy were still far behind. The water around them heaved as the Mosasaurus swam around in circles, slowly honing in on them. Sammy's panicked eyes met Yasmina's.

"No," Yasmina said. She stopped paddling and stared up at a crane platform. Crouching, she scooped up Bumpy and plopped her into the spot Yasmina had just vacated. Then Yasmina took Bumpy's spot.

"What are you doing?" Ben shouted.

"Whatever you do, don't stop paddling!" Yasmina ordered, and then she grabbed her metal paddle and pulled herself up onto the crane platform.

From her vantage point on the platform, Yasmina could see the Mosasaurus closing in on Darius and

Sammy. She banged the paddle on the platform as hard as she could. WHANG!

The sound echoed throughout the lagoon.

Brooklynn and Kenji had made it up the ladder and into the safety of the spectator stands. They helped Ben and Bumpy up and called for Darius and Sammy to hurry.

The Mosasaurus was almost upon them!

"Don't look back, Sammy!" Darius said frantically. "Just keep paddling!"

"I'm tryin', but—what's Yaz doin'?"

The Mosasaurus was getting nearer and nearer as Darius raised his head. He saw Yasmina on the platform, banging her paddle.

"Hey! Hey!" Yasmina shouted. "Over here! Hey!"

"She's distracting it, buying us time!" Darius said. "Keep going!"

"We gotta do something!" Sammy yelled as they reached the stands.

Thinking fast, Kenji ran off and started up the feeding crane.

Yasmina looked up and saw the chain coming her way. She jumped onto it, holding the chain tightly as it swung her back toward the others.

The Mosasaurus was now in pursuit as the crane moved back to the spectator stands. The dinosaur was picking up speed. It was familiar with the chain. The chain brought its food every day. And there was something on the chain.

"She's not gonna make it!" Kenji screamed.

As the Mosasaurus breeched the water's surface, just about to take a bite, Yasmina swung forward on the chain. The Mosasaurus missed by inches!

Chomping down, its massive jaws snapped the crane cable instead, and the Mosasaurus sunk back into the water below.

The crane arm continued to inch Yasmina—who was hanging on to the chain for dear life—toward the stands. As soon as she was over the stands, Yasmina fell, her left ankle hitting the ground hard. She screamed in pain.

Sammy rushed to her friend's side.

"Thank you," Sammy said, sitting down next to Yasmina. The athletic girl winced as she touched her left ankle ever so slightly. She was used to aches and pains, but this was different.

"For saving us," Sammy continued. "For saving me. That was amazing. *You're* amazing."

"Stop," Yasmina said, standing up, grimacing at the pain. "We may need each other to stay alive, but don't think for a second that makes us friends again."

Yasmina turned away, doing her best to disguise her limp. Sammy frowned and drew her knees up close to her chest.

"You okay?"

Sammy looked surprised as Brooklynn sat down next to her.

"Naw. Not really."

"Yeah, dumb question," Brooklynn said. "I don't know her that well, but I think if you give Yaz some space, she'll come around."

"Why are you being nice to me?" Sammy asked.

"Because I've done my share of selfish things," Brooklynn said. "I only knew what you were up to because I was also sneaking in places I shouldn't have been. You were at least doing it for family. I was doing it to impress a bunch of angry internet randos."

A look of determination came over Brooklynn's face. "Plus, when we get out of here, you're gonna give *me* the exclusive on all the juicy details of you spying for Mantah Corp. 'Brooklynn Unboxes a

Conspiracy.' Try to tell me my videos are lame after *that,* angry internet randos!!"

Sammy looked into Brooklynn's eyes.

"So . . . deal?" Brooklynn said, putting out her hand. Sammy grinned. She took the other girl's hand. They shook.

Then came the sirens.

CHAPTER TWELVE

"**A**ttention!" a voice said over the PA. "All park-goers must report to the south ferry dock for immediate evacuation. Last ferry departs in ninety minutes."

"We have to move," Darius said. "The only way we're going to make it is if we run."

Sammy nodded in Yasmina's direction, catching Darius's attention. He saw her hunched over, rubbing her injured ankle.

Yasmina started to walk, but Darius could see that it was a painful effort.

"Are you sure that's the best way to get there?" Sammy asked.

Suddenly, Yasmina straightened up. "I'm *fine,*" she said sharply. "I've competed with a torn ACL. You should be way more worried about Ben and Bumpy."

"What we should *all* be worried about is catching a boat out of here, and, naturally, we have a problem," Ben said. He zipped open his fanny pack and pulled out one of the kids' placemat maps from the common room. Ben flipped the placemat over, revealing a printed map of the island.

"We're here," he said, pointing, "and the docks are on the southern tip of the island. Even if we ran at peak Yaz speed, there's no way we'd make the last boat out."

"You don't know that," Sammy said, hoping he didn't.

"Yes, I do," Ben said. "I memorized the evacuation plan on the ferry ride over."

"Okay," Darius said, regrouping. "So we need another way. Can we use those kayaks? Or send the fastest one of us to run and tell the ferry people to wait?"

Darius peered into the sky and flinched as a flash of light caught his eye. Then there was a soft sound—a whooshing noise—and it seemed to be coming closer. Looking at the elevated track above the Mosasaurus lagoon, Darius saw it—the Jurassic World monorail! It could take them all the way to the ferry docks!

They were already heading up the stairs that would take them to the approaching monorail when Toro arrived.

Brooklynn saw him first and shushed everyone,

making a frantic "GET DOWN!" motion with her hands.

Darius turned his head, looking below. Toro was by the monorail stairs, sniffing as if he had caught the scent of prey. Darius locked eyes with the group. He whispered, "Move. Fast."

Crouching, the group stayed down below the railing, trying to avoid the Carnotaurus's field of vision.

So far, so good.

Kenji made it to the top of the stairs just as the monorail pulled into the station. But a roar from below let the group know that the Carnotaurus had found them.

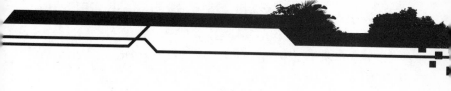

CHAPTER THIRTEEN

"**R**UN!" Darius screamed as the monorail slowed down and came to a stop. Its doors opened. Everyone sprinted across the platform for the monorail.

The monorail's doors were already closing, and Toro was coming!

Below them, Toro attempted to force his way up the stairs to catch his prey. But the stairs were far too narrow for the dinosaur's massive frame. Darius gasped as he saw the dinosaur coming closer.

Yasmina struggled on her injured ankle.

Darius hurried to her and threw her arm over his shoulder, taking some of the weight off her bad ankle. With the Carnotaurus approaching, they finally made it to the top. They raced across the platform, where they found Kenji and Brooklynn holding the monorail doors open—

"Please stand clear of the closing doors," the PA insisted.

"Hurry!" Brooklynn cried.

As Darius and Yasmina leaped through the monorail doors, they saw Toro lunge! But the stairs collapsed beneath his monstrous weight, and the platform crumbled.

As the monorail zoomed along the tracks, Darius stared out the window, his mind drifting. He caught sight of Jurassic World in a state of complete disarray and destruction. Smoke drifted skyward, flames burning bright below.

Turning to the others, Darius said, "Guys. We did it. We're going home."

"This calls for a celebration!" Brooklynn said.

"I cannot *wait* to be home," Yasmina said. "Once my ankle's better, it's back to training. And I guess finding a new corporate sponsor since mine *was* Jurassic World."

Darius almost laughed.

"It's gonna be weird for things to be normal again," he said. "Like, are video games gonna seem boring now?"

Kenji laughed.

"How about you?" Darius asked, looking at Kenji. "What's the first thing you'll do when you get home?"

"Depends on which wing of our mansion you're talkin' 'bout," Kenji said. "East wing's usually off limits, but Dad and Candy are away on business, so . . . I guess I'll go downstairs to our bowling alley. Staff always lets me win. Life of a VIP."

"So," Sammy said, changing the subject. "What have you missed, Ben?"

The kids kept on talking, sharing what they would do once they got home and weren't being chased by dinosaurs and being faced with an all-encompassing, impending doom.

Everything was going to be fine.

Until the thunderous boom in the distance and the sudden shaking made them all realize it wasn't.

The kids looked out of the monorail windows, but they couldn't really see anything other than the sky filled with thick, black smoke and an orange, flickering glow beneath it.

Of course, that was the direction in which the monorail was heading.

"It sounded like an explosion," Yasmina said.

"I don't think it was near us," Darius said, quietly

hoping he was right. "We're okay. We're still okay."

Trying to brighten the mood again, Sammy said, "I know camp wasn't what we thought it was gonna be. But after everything we went through, at least we're leaving this place with five new friends."

This was followed by an awkward silence.

"Wait. Do you guys not see us as friends?"

"I mean, doesn't it usually take more than a few days to become friends with someone?" Brooklynn asked.

"We were thrown together at random, and we have *nothing* in common," Yasmina said.

"That's not true!" Sammy protested. "We've been through more together than most friends have in a lifetime!"

"And now that it's over, what are the odds that we'll ever see each other again?" Ben wondered.

The monorail car grew quiet as each kid realized that Ben was probably right.

The silence was broken by the sound of the park announcer over the PA.

"Coming up on the right, you'll see our world-renowned eighteen-hole dinosaur-themed golf course. It's one of the many wonders that makes this park so very *Jurassic*."

Brooklynn looked up at the PA and scrunched her nose. "What does that even mean?"

"I thought I knew," Darius said. "My whole life, I

had this idea of Jurassic World. My dad used to say this place was 'Allosaurus and a bag of chips.' He was so corny."

Brooklynn looked at Darius and turned her head slightly. "Um . . . 'was'? So your dad is . . . ?"

Darius nodded.

"Dang it!"

Everyone turned to see Ben rummaging through his fanny pack as he talked to himself. "Come on, it's gotta be here somewhere. . . . Bumpy stepped in something icky, and I'm low on sanitizer. It's fine. I can make more."

From his fanny pack, Ben produced small bottles of aloe vera and rubbing alcohol.

"Ben, *why are you here*?" Kenji finally asked.

Darius shot Kenji a look. "What he means is, well, you're scared of dinosaurs. And the outdoors. And sometimes the indoors. And germs."

"My mom works for Mr. Masrani," Ben said. "She got me into camp. Said it would be a great way for me to 'face my fears.' It's been a nightmare! I'm sick of being scared all the time. And of running, and of almost getting eaten, and . . . and of holding everyone back. I just can't do . . . this."

Bumpy mewed quietly, looking at Ben. Then he smiled. "But it's not all bad. If I hadn't come, I never would have met—"

WHAM!!!

Something smashed into the monorail window.

Bumpy squealed.

The kids jumped back, recoiling as they saw a winged Pteranodon thrashing against the glass. The creature slipped from view as the monorail continued down the track.

Then they heard a pecking sound.

Behind them, they could see a dark cloud rapidly approaching. But it wasn't a cloud.

It was a *flock* of Pteranodons!

Something's attracting the Pteranodons, Darius thought. *But what?*

Then he looked up at the ceiling, at the bright lights inside the monorail car.

"We gotta turn off the lights!" Darius shouted. "Flying reptiles are basically seabirds! They're attracted to shiny, moving objects, and with all these lights on—"

"*We're* a shiny, moving object!" Sammy gasped.

At once, everyone started to smash the lights. Soon, the rear monorail car was dark.

Darius slid open the door that connected the rear car to the one in front of it. Wind hit his face as he stepped through the narrow corridor into the car.

"Brooklynn! You're with Yaz," he directed.

"Sammy, help Ben and Bumpy across!"

The Pteranodons had almost reached the monorail as Darius and the others ran, smashing lights along the way. Everyone had made it into the next car. Sammy looked out the window and gasped. There was a stopped monorail on the tracks. Not just stopped, though. Destroyed. Pteranodons attacked it like it was some pitiful, wounded animal.

"At least now we know what that boom was earlier," Sammy said.

"If we don't switch tracks or stop this car right now, we're going to hit that thing, full speed!" Darius said.

Kenji pointed to the door ahead. "The front car—there's control panels there! VIP tour—I was eight, they let me drive!"

Darius ran to the door, but it wouldn't open. "No, no, no!" Darius said, rattling the handle, trying to force it open. The other kids joined him, but it was no use.

Kenji tried to smash the window, but that wouldn't break.

Darius peered through the window into the car. He saw the control panel, and then something caught his eye. There was a small emergency hatch just above the panel. His eyes drifted back into the car he was in, and Darius saw a similar small hatch in the ceiling above him.

Pointing to the hatch, he said, "I'm gonna get to the control car through there."

"You can't go there!" Kenji said. "That's where the flying whatevers are!"

"We don't have a choice! Me and—"

Darius looked at Ben, the only other person who could possibly fit through the hatch. Ben was cowering.

"I'm the only one who can fit!"

BAM! The monorail suddenly shook.

Ben comforted a whimpering Bumpy, and he looked at the frightened kids around him.

"Distract the flock while I crawl over the top to the control car," Darius said. "Use the flashlights, just keep them away from—"

All eyes suddenly turned to see Ben's legs as he disappeared through the hatch.

CHAPTER FOURTEEN

"**B**en!" Darius shouted out the hatch. "Ben, what are you doing?"

He reached his hand out, but Ben refused. "I can do this! Just distract them!"

Ben turned and saw a Pteranodon flying right in his direction. Darius ducked back into the car. "Come on! We have to keep them away from Ben!"

The kids ran to different windows of the monorail, each person armed with an emergency flashlight they had grabbed from the monorail cars. They started waving the flashlights out the windows, the bright lights distracting the Pteranodon bearing down on Ben.

The creature suddenly changed course, no longer going after Ben.

It was coming after *them.*

Atop the monorail, Ben wobbled, unsteady. The wind whipped at him, and he struggled to hang on.

He crawled ahead, slowly making his way toward the control car hatch.

Closing his eyes, Ben took a deep, long breath.

"I can do this," he said to himself. "I can do this!"

Inching closer and closer along the roof of the monorail, Ben at last reached the hatch. He pushed hard on the latch, and it opened with a loud POP.

He drew himself toward the hatch and jumped inside the control car.

The control panel was completely confusing, row upon row of lights and buttons. Ben had no idea what was connected to what or what did what or anything.

The only thing he understood was a photograph of a younger Kenji that had been attached to the dashboard with the words BANNED FROM MONORAIL TOURS written beneath it.

Ben started to randomly press buttons. He could hear the Pteranodons outside, slamming into the monorail's back cars. Then he put his hand on a lever and pulled it. Suddenly, the monorail veered to the left, switching over to a new track.

The monorail shook as the rear car clipped the stopped train and flew off the tracks. Ben looked out the window as he heard an explosion below. Ben could no longer hear the Pteranodons outside—they must have been distracted by the explosion!

Behind him, the other kids started hammering on

the window and chanting, "BEN! BEN! BEN!"

Ben pressed the button opening the door between the control car and the one behind it.

"You saved us, Ben!" Darius said proudly. "I didn't know you had it in—"

Before Darius could finish his sentence, a Pteranodon smashed through the window of the control car. It grabbed Ben and dragged him out of the car.

The Pteranodon dropped Ben, and he was now dangling out of the monorail as Darius reached through the smashed window. Darius grabbed the boy's small hand.

"Hold on, Ben!" Darius said, his grip slipping.

"I can't!"

WHAM!

The monorail suddenly hit another patch of bad track, and then Darius lost his grip completely.

Ben fell into the dark jungle below. Darius could only watch in horror as the small boy plummeted and two Pteranodons swooped down after him.

The monorail moved so quickly that in seconds it felt like Ben and the moment when he had been in the control car had never existed. Darius stood there, too stunned to cry . . . or feel anything. Brooklynn put her hand on his shoulder. Yasmina was shocked, holding Sammy in her arms.

Kenji held Ben's fanny pack.

Bumpy wailed.

"He's gone," Yasmina said. "He's . . . *gone.*"

"No!" Sammy screamed.

Darius looked away from the jungle and to the monorail behind him. Then he turned, gazing out the windshield.

"We're going back," Darius said flatly.

Everyone turned to look at him.

"The monorail is going back!"

The monorail shimmied, and the kids were thrown off balance. Darius saw the lights of the dock, which had only just become visible, disappear.

"When we switched tracks, we ended up on one headed north. We're not going to the south docks," Darius explained. "We're going *away* from them!"

Darius looked at the control panel and started pressing buttons and pulling levers.

But nothing happened.

WHAM!

Everyone was thrown to the floor of the control car as the monorail sailed over more bad track. Sparks flew as the speeding monorail bucked wildly.

"We gotta get off the monorail, now!" Darius yelled.

Brooklynn pointed out the smashed window.

"The track dips down up ahead! We can jump there!"

Darius raced to the side door. With great effort, he and Sammy opened it.

Kenji strapped on Ben's fanny pack, grabbed hold of Bumpy, and as the car lurched again, the kids jumped.

They hit the ground hard and rolled down a grassy hillside. Darius was amazed that he was still in one piece.

"Bumpy!" Kenji said, looking worried. "Where's Bumpy? I lost her when I hit the ground. She's gotta be here. Bumpy? *Bumpy!*"

"Shhhh!" Brooklynn said. "There are still dinosaurs out here, including Toro and—"

"BUMPY!" Kenji screamed, ignoring Brooklynn.

"We gotta look for her, don't we? And Ben and—"

"How?" Yasmina said curtly. "We don't even know where we—"

A siren blared, interrupting her. Then the sound of an urgent voice over the PA: "Attention. All park-goers must report to the south ferry dock for immediate evacuation. Last ferry departs in one hour."

Darius looked at the group. "*We* can make it to the ferry. But only if we go *now*."

Kenji's eyes opened wide. "But . . ."

"I know, Kenji," Darius said. "We have to go."

Kenji looked down at the fanny pack around his waist.

The kids sprinted through the jungle, moving through the thick brush. Sammy looked over her shoulder and saw Yasmina limping, trying to move as fast as she could given her injury. Sammy was about to say something when Yasmina twisted her ankle, falling.

Everyone rushed to her side as Brooklynn looked at Yasmina's now very swollen ankle. The injured girl tried to push her away.

"How are you even walking?" Brooklynn asked.

"Last ferry departs in forty-five minutes," came the voice over the PA.

"I'm . . . highly motivated," Yasmina said, mastering her pain with a deep breath.

"She can't keep up like this," Sammy said, looking at Darius. "What do we do?"

"The tunnels!" Darius shouted. "Kenji! The maintenance tunnels. There has to be one that leads to the docks, right? Kenji? Right?"

Kenji thought about it for a moment, and then his face lit up.

The maintenance tunnel was darker than Darius remembered, and the day's events had him—and everyone—on edge.

"This'll get us to the dock in half the time!" Kenji said as he took the lead.

"Are we sure Mr. VIP knows what he's doing?" Brooklynn asked.

"Kenji took me down here before," Darius answered. "Just trust him. We'll be outta here in . . ." And then they turned a corner and hit a dead end. ". . . no time."

All eyes were on Kenji as he squirmed. "Everything looks different with the lights all freaky like this, okay?"

Then Kenji snapped his fingers and said, "I remember now! This way!"

Then he ran off. A second later, he was back and running in the opposite direction.

"Guess it's this way," Darius said, and the unconvinced group followed.

"This wasn't here before!" Kenji said as they ran into a large metal grate separating the tunnel.

"It's okay. We'll go another way," Darius said, trying to stay positive.

A moment later, they reached another dead end. They tried another tunnel that ended in a locked door. Kenji pulled, but it wouldn't open.

Darius noticed that there were lockers lining the wall. Brooklynn yanked one door open, and something fell out.

A stun spear!

"We can use this for—" Brooklynn started, just as Kenji grabbed the spear. He brought the sparking tip of the stun spear to the metal door handle, which was a really bad idea, because he got an electric shock and fell to the floor.

"I'm fine," Kenji said.

"Attention," came the voice over the park PA, "all park-goers must report to the south ferry dock for immediate evacuation. Last ferry departs in thirty minutes."

"Uh, Kenji, Darius?" Sammy said. "The way we came from . . . where does that tunnel end?"

"It opens up into the Park, I guess. Why?" Kenji asked.

Then they turned to look where Sammy had been focused, and they saw a huge shadow cast on the tunnel wall. The shadow of a dinosaur.

CHAPTER FIFTEEN

Darius could hear his heart beating in his ears, louder than anything he'd heard before.

The kids had thrown themselves against the sides of the tunnels and weren't making a sound. They watched in silent terror as the shadow grew closer.

It was a dinosaur, all right. A turkey-sized Compsognathus.

Suddenly, shoulders eased, and everyone relaxed.

"It's like a foot tall!" Brooklynn said, giggling.

"And, uh, not alone," Yasmina said. She pointed behind the Compy as another Compsognathus appeared. Then another. And another. Soon, a group of tiny dinosaurs had assembled.

"We need to go," Darius said. "In a group, Compys can—"

"Not really the time for a lesson, Dino Nerd!" Kenji said sharply.

"Why not?" Brooklynn said. "It's not like you've gotten us anywhere even close to the dock, Mr. VIP!"

"Oh, I'm sorry," Kenji said. "Don't you have some sort of 'Unboxing Being a Brat All the Time' video to be shooting?"

"Hey!" Sammy shouted. "Y'all calm yourselves. You're scaring the itty-bitty Compy family."

"GUYS!" Darius screamed. "Just stop!"

He looked over to see the Compys all frozen in place, unmoving. The tiny dinosaurs looked back at the tunnel from where they'd emerged, then took off running in the other direction.

There was a loud roar coming from the tunnel now, and as the lights flickered, the kids could see the shape of a large dinosaur coming for them.

"Toro!" Darius shouted.

Kenji looked at the stun spear in his hands, then tossed it to Yasmina. Then he sprinted down another tunnel.

"*Now* you know which way to go?" Brooklynn said in amazement.

Toro took off down the tunnel, chasing after the kids. As they rounded a corner, so, too, did the Carnotaurus. But he couldn't take the corners as fast as they could. The huge dinosaur slammed into a tunnel wall, momentarily dazed. The creature stalked down the tunnel, still searching for his prey as he passed by a grate on the wall.

"We can't stay here!" Sammy whispered from inside the grate. "The ferry—"

Kenji shushed her.

Yasmina turned her head and nudged Darius. There was a metal plate against the back of the vent wall.

She wedged the tip of the stun spear between the wall and the plate. With effort, she and Darius were able to use it as a lever and finally pry open the grate. Inside was a small opening. It wasn't very big . . . but maybe it would be big enough for one kid to fit through at a time.

Darius was about to get everyone's attention when, suddenly, Toro's head smashed through the outside vent!

"Go-go-go!" Darius shouted over the screaming of the kids. Grabbing the stun spear from Yasmina, Darius watched the other kids go down the small opening while he jabbed at the Carnotaurus.

With the others safely inside, Darius thrust the stun spear at Toro again, this time striking him right in the large, painful-looking gash that he had received in their first encounter. The dinosaur roared in pain as Darius got away.

"Attention. All park-goers must report to the south ferry dock for immediate evacuation. Last ferry departs in fifteen minutes."

Darius heard the voice over the PA just as he fell from the vent to the floor of a new tunnel.

He got to his feet and was stunned to see the other kids were there, smiling at him.

"Why are you—" Darius started to say.

Smiling, Brooklynn pointed to a nearby sign on a wall. The sign had an arrow with the words EXIT TO SOUTH DOCK—1,000 FEET.

The kids ran down the tunnel, turned around a corner, and found themselves in a large room with a high ceiling. The center of the ceiling appeared to be sunken a bit, a monorail track running through it. Crates lined the walls of the room, stacked one on top of the other. Darius spotted a cart with wheels to one side.

This was all fine, but Darius felt his heart sink when he saw that the corridor that *should* lead to the docks was completely sealed off by concrete.

"There's gotta be a door or—" Darius said.

"There's not," Brooklynn said. "There's no way out. They must've sealed it off after the Park was finished!"

Yasmina threw the stun spear to the ground angrily. "Can't *anyone* associated with this place make just *one* good decision?"

As if in response, the Carnotaurus roared, still on the hunt for them.

"Darius . . . what do we do now?" Kenji asked. One by one, the kids all turned to face Darius.

"I don't know," Darius said quietly, sitting down. "I don't know what to do. I didn't know what to do about Ben . . . or Bumpy . . . or when the Indominus rex attacked. I didn't even know how to make *regular* camp work! All I did was tell bad stories and get into trouble and mess up everything."

He put his head in his hands. "You never should have trusted me. I should've just stayed home. I'm a dino nerd who played a video game, and I'm no good at any of this."

He was surprised to find Kenji next to him.

"But you are," Kenji said. "Good at this. None of us would have known what to do, Darius. But because *you* didn't give up, we didn't give up, either."

Sammy looked at Darius, smiling. "You kept us going, no matter what."

"You made us feel like we were in this together,"

Yasmina said. "So we are. We're a team. We're *your* team."

Then Brooklynn sat down beside him. "Things fall apart. And that's okay. Because when that happens . . ."

Darius looked at Brooklynn. "We pick up the pieces, and we keep going."

Darius stood up as Toro roared, closer than before.

"Let's see what's in these crates," Darius said.

"Medical supplies," Kenji said as he lifted a handful of bandages from a crate. "Well, at least our luck is consistent."

The other kids were opening crates, too, and each was finding only different kinds of medical supplies. Plenty of tape, bandages, and cotton balls.

ROAR. Closer now.

Nothing pointy or good for making a Carnotaurus go away.

"Now what?" Yasmina asked. "We wrap ourselves up like mummies and scare him to death?"

"Or give him a bunch of this oxygen and hope he gets light-headed," Kenji said.

"Wait, what?" Darius asked. He ran over to Kenji

and looked into the crate filled with oxygen tanks.

"Check it. Oxygen tanks for days," Kenji said.

"Supercompressed air, sensitive to pressure and heat," Darius said.

"Might be able to scare Toro off," Brooklynn said.

"Or distract him long enough for us to find another exit," Darius added.

"Cool, cool," Yasmina said. "So we makin' the boom-boom or what?"

Darius turned and saw the wheeled cart he had noticed earlier.

"Kenji and Brooklynn, let's get this crate loaded on the cart. Sammy, use those bandages and tape to make a fuse. We're gonna need something to light it with."

Yasmina smiled at Darius as she raised the stun spear. Sparks shot from the tip, and Darius grinned.

Toro entered the huge room, angry, roaring. There was no sign of his prey anywhere.

That's because they were behind the cart filled with oxygen tanks, finishing their science project.

"Light it up," Darius whispered.

Yasmina touched the tip of the stun spear to the makeshift fuse that Sammy had cobbled together.

It wouldn't light.

Darius peered over the cart and saw the Carnotaurus turn in their direction.

He must have heard me whispering! Darius thought.

Ducking down, his eyes grew wide. "This really needs to happen right now!"

"Wait!" Kenji interjected. Then he unzipped Ben's fanny pack and started riffling through it.

The Carnotaurus took a huge step closer.

Then Kenji pulled out "Hand sanitizer! This stuff will burn!"

Kenji poured the sanitizer on the fuse, and Yasmina touched the tip of the stun spear to it again. This time, it ignited.

"Thanks, Ben," Brooklynn said.

"NOW!" Darius shouted.

The kids jumped out from behind the cart as the Carnotaurus took another step forward. The fuse was burning, and the kids pushed the cart right for the furious Toro!

Flames licked the sides of the crate, rapidly engulfing it.

"Come on, come on," Darius said impatiently.

As the cart reached the Carnotaurus, the dinosaur simply kicked it aside. The crate shattered and the oxygen tanks scattered across the room, along with flaming crate debris.

So far, in terms of things not going to plan, the

plan was working perfectly. The flaming debris had set the other crates on fire, and now the kids faced double jeopardy—the Carnotaurus on one horrible hand and fiery doom on the other.

CHAPTER SIXTEEN

The Carnotaurus charged right at the kids, but they managed to dive out of the way in time. Darius grabbed Yasmina by the arm, pulling her along. Yasmina winced in pain.

It was impossible to find a hiding spot. No sooner would someone duck behind a flaming crate than the angry Carnotaurus would charge forward, swipe his tail, and shatter the box.

Not knowing what else to do, the kids tried to scramble over the depression in the center of the room, the one that held the monorail track. The Carnotaurus's jaws were snapping open and closed, open and closed as the kids managed their way onto the depression.

First Kenji made it, then Brooklynn.

Sammy was next.

Yasmina screamed in pain from her ankle. The stun spear was in her hands. She looked the

Carnotaurus right in the eye.

Just as the dinosaur was about to attack her, Darius hurled a flaming board at the Carnotaurus, hitting the creature right in its festering scar. The burning board caused the dinosaur to rear back in pain.

This was Yasmina's chance!

She made the leap for the depression and would have missed—if it wasn't for Sammy. The other girl caught her arms and pulled her up.

"Thanks," Yasmina said to Sammy.

But it wasn't over yet. Darius was still down there with a really, really angry Carnotaurus.

"Jump!" Kenji screamed.

As Toro approached, Darius ran, getting ready to make his leap.

Except the Carnotaurus lunged at the same moment! The dinosaur caught the back of his foot, and Darius tumbled down below.

Darius was in a daze and could hardly see straight. He was on his back, and he saw Toro looking at him, leaning, getting closer. The furious creature was coming in for the kill—but stepped on some stray oxygen tanks. The Carnotaurus stumbled, losing his footing. Trying to right himself, he stepped on the edge of the depression, which caused him to tumble right toward Darius!

Coming to his senses, Darius rolled, and the dinosaur fell down right next to him. Toro thrashed.

Darius could feel the creatures's awful breath on him as Kenji reached down. Darius grabbed his hand, and Kenji hauled him up.

Below, Toro was getting back on his feet.

It wasn't over yet.

Darius and Yasmina looked at each other as they noticed the oxygen tanks rolling around on the ground by the Carnotaurus. Then they looked at the stun spear in Yasmina's hands. She handed it to Darius with a nod to say "good luck." He activated the weapon and locked the switch. The stun spear sparked madly.

"See you on the other side, VIP," Darius said, giving Kenji a devilish look.

"Meet ya there, Dino Nerd," Kenji replied.

The Carnotaurus roared as Darius hurled the spear right at an oxygen tank.

The explosion knocked the kids off their feet, and the heat from below almost scorched them.

It was quiet following the explosion. The kids stared below, watching the smoke rise.

"We did it! We beat—" Kenji said.

"No—look!" Sammy said, pointing below.

They heard shifting rubble as a shadowy shape began to rise from the smoke.

It was Toro. Burned. Bruised. Battered.

But the kids weren't afraid. If this was the end, so be it. They would go down fighting.

Maybe the Carnotaurus could sense this? Because instead of attacking, the wounded creature looked up at the kids, then turned away. Toro limped back down the tunnel from which he had come.

"It doesn't get better than that," Darius said, smiling.

"Wanna bet?" Yasmina said with an enormous grin plastered across her face. She pointed at the wall—the explosion had blasted a hole through it!

They scrambled into the sunlight and raced toward the docks. They still had a ways to go, but hope kept them going. Soon, the docks came into view, and . . . they were empty.

They had missed the last ferry.

"They'll be back for us, won't they?" Sammy asked as they stared out over the water.

"Of course they will," Darius said reassuringly. "And until then . . . we've got each other."

The kids stood together on the dock, watching as the sun came up over the horizon. Brooklynn hugged

Sammy and Yasmina as Kenji punched Darius playfully on the arm. Darius smiled.

Darius thought back to the story he was trying to tell the other kids, back at the camp, back before everything fell apart.

"We thought it'd be fun," Darius said, sitting down. It seemed like ages since he had been off his feet. "We thought we'd be safe. But we didn't realize the horror waiting for us on the island. Claws . . . teeth . . . screaming. So much screaming. But we'll keep fighting. That's the promise we make every day we get. That despite all the hardships, you never give up. We will survive. We *will* get home. Because no matter what happens . . . no matter what this place throws at us next . . . none of us are in this alone."